Vernella Fuller was born in St Catherine, Jamaica, in 1956, the second of six children. She moved to England at the age of twelve to join her parents. She went to secondary school in South London, received her first degree from Sussex University, a postgraduate teaching certificate from Goldsmiths College, London University and an MA from the institute of Education, London University. She taught for ten years at a London comprehensive and is currently a Senior Lecturer at Southwark College.

Vernella has one daughter, Alisha, and is guardian to a seventeen-year-old, Julie. She has a passion for good food, travelling, yoga and cricket.

Going Back Home is her first novel. She is currently working on her second.

D0995832

VERNELLA FULLER

Going Back Home

First published by The Women's Press Ltd 1992
A member of the Namara Group
34 Great Sutton Street, London EC1V 0DX

British Library Cataloguing in Publication Data
A catalogue record for this book is available from the
British Library.

ISBN 0 7043 4301 0

Typeset by Contour Typesetters, Southall, London
Printed and bound in Great Britain by
BPCC Hazells Ltd
Member of BPCC Ltd

ACKNOWLEDGEMENTS

I would like to acknowledge Joan Riley whose encouragement, support and advice on various aspects of the earlier draft kept me writing; Ken, Maureen and Chris for their encouragement; Alisha Nadine who, despite herself, allowed me time to write; Kathy Gale who spent many hours helping me to shape and refine the text. Her perceptive and constructive comments were indispensable.

To my family, especially my daughter, Alisha.

Prologue

Joy stood in the sun, one arm on the bus shelter the other akimbo. It was hot for that time of the morning, the gentle breeze making no impact on the heat. At least three minibuses had passed, going in the opposite direction to Spanish Town, and providing constant amusement to Joy. A variety of limbs protruded from their windows; arms, legs, heads, even bottoms seemingly glued to where the doors should have been as the buses sped past the petrol station and round the bend.

The smell of frying onions, waiting impatiently in pans for callaloo or ackee and saltfish, made Joy regret that she had only had tea before leaving home. She inhaled deeply, breathing in the smells, the sights and sounds. There was so much to absorb. The hibiscus edges surrounding the white bungalows, their elegant canopies warding off the fiercest heat from the verandas. The big mango tree by the corner well laden with green fruits and the odd yellow one, half-hidden among the leaves; the coconut trees regal in the distance, the limes proudly rooted.

'Yams, sweet potatoes, dasheen, callaloo . . . That's what me a sell . . . Yams, sweet potatoes . . . dasheen, callaloo . . .', a barefoot woman sang at the top of her voice as she passed with a basket on her head, her hands swinging by her side.

The radios, some blaring out RJR, others JBC, competed for pre-eminence. There was a hold-up on the Marcus Garvey Drive,

Joy heard, the way they were headed. Somebody's car had fallen into a pot-hole and had come out without one of its wheels. The heavy pounding of the reggae she adored serenaded her from the house behind her, rivalling the clash of pans, screams of mothers to children to *sweep the yard, hurry up* with this or that, cocooning Joy in an immense feeling of well-being.

Esmine stood underneath the bus shelter shifting about restlessly, squinting against the glare of the sun. She put on her sun-glasses, almost breaking them in her irritation. They slid down her sweaty nose. She grabbed them off and jammed them in the side of her bag. The constant dust was getting into her eyes. She dreaded the thought of the way her clothes must look. Her hair! She daren't open her mouth for fear that one of the countless flies would go down her throat. And the noise. The radios, car horns, the clamour from kitchens and yards. She couldn't understand why it had to be so loud!

She wanted to spit. The scent from the drain behind the bus stop, with its stagnant water and left-over jerk pork and chicken mingled with the smell of breakfast, cooking in too much oil. It turned her stomach. Her relief when she saw the minibus finally speeding round the bend towards them. It was enormous. But then she saw how packed it was. She gritted her teeth as it screeched to a halt, and followed Joy towards it, failing to avoid contact with the sweaty bodies that swarmed around them from out of nowhere. They found a seat just before the bus sped off, neither of them speaking for a long time.

'I could live here you know Esmine. I love it,' Joy said finally, breaking their silence and ignoring the vexed look on her sister's face.

The minibus jolted, unbalancing the man whose stale armpit had been pressed against Joy's cheek. He fell heavily on her, managed to pull himself up and smiled a toothless apology.

Esmine squeezed herself against the side of the bus and grabbed

2

the seat in front of her as they sped round another bend. 'What?'

Joy raised her voice over the rattling engine and other conversations. 'I said I could live here!'

Esmine ran her hand through her hair, hopelessly battling with the breeze to keep it in place.

Joy grinned, 'I told you that you were wasting your time with that fancy style.'

Esmine tutted, 'God I can't believe it.' She tried again to smooth her hair, giving up finally in disgust. 'I only had the stupid thing done a week ago. And look at this T-shirt.' She pulled the damp cotton away from her chest. 'It's soaking. I'm a mess.' She fanned her face with her open palm. 'God it's hot . . . I should know better than to follow you.'

Joy shrugged. 'Don't be such a baby, Esmine. You should have pinned your hair up as I said.' She gave her cane rows a smug pat. 'See, mine's fine.'

Esmine's frown deepened, 'I should have gone in the car with Mummy and Daddy.' She glanced up at the gap above her head that was supposed to be a window.

'Esmine, just shut up and let me take in the scene.'

Esmine sighed.

'Anyway, you need the experience, travelling like this. It's wonderful.'

'Speak for yourself,' Esmine snapped.

Joy looked around the minibus. 'Oh Esmine I feel so good.' She shook her legs. 'The heat and all these people chatting and laughing. This is home . . .'

Esmine tutted and sighed. 'Joy, be quiet and stop shaking yourself up. You're making me hot and bothered.'

Joy leaned across and kissed her sister on the cheek. 'Just let yourself go Esmine and force yourself to enjoy it . . .' she smiled.

Esmine tried to hold on to her irritation but Joy's mood was infectious. She smiled too.

3

The bus screeched to a halt. Several people pushed their way to the front and out of the bus. Esmine's eyes widened as more people got on and those on the bus shifted and rearranged themselves to make room.

'One stap driver,' a large woman who had somehow managed to push through to the front shouted as the driver accelerated at speed away from the bus stop.

Esmine sucked air through her teeth as Joy's toothless neighbour perched himself on the edge of the seat. 'You don't mind do you dahta?'

Joy covered her mouth with her hand to squeeze the laughter back and shook her head. She turned to Esmine for diversion.

Esmine shook her head, 'I can't believe they just let all those people on.'

Joy gave her sister an embarrassed look, conscious of the man bouncing against her as the bus fell in and out of a pot-hole. 'Keep your voice down will you,' she muttered under her breath; 'don't advertise the fact that you come from *farign*'.

'Very funny. You can pretend as much as you like but I'm proud of it.'

'Proud of *what*?'

'Who's shouting now?'

Joy tried to control her irritation, 'I *said* proud of what?'

'No shout at de pretty little dahta like dat.' The man perched at the edge of her seat looked at Joy then across at Esmine with a satisfied smile.

Esmine fingered her earring and looked out of the window. Joy mumbled under her breath and frowned.

Esmine turned back to her, lowering her voice, 'Joy, you aren't Jamaican so just give it a rest.'

Joy was determined not to let her have the last word. 'Sometimes I wonder about you, you know Esmine. Daddy would . . .'

'*Stop quoting Daddy to me!*' Esmine glared at her, a long-standing bitterness surfacing. 'If you're not careful you'll get as crazy as

4

him, living in some stupid dream about Jamaica the promised land. Just look around Joy.' She gestured at the broken down shacks flashing past the window and the women selling by the roadside, 'What kind of promised land is all that? . . .'

'Nobody said it was perfect,' Joy said quietly.

'I've just had enough of the two of you going on and on. If you can't see what this place is really about . . . how far from your dream it is, then you are more stupid than I thought.'

Joy bit her lip. 'And everyone thinks you are so quiet and sweet. Well all I can say is that I feel sorry for you; you may have got nine grade As at O level but you are still as thick as a plank.'

'Typical, if all else fails, insult.'

Joy made a face and folded her arms, aware that her sister was right but resenting her comment anyway.

Esmine grinned suddenly and kissed Joy on the cheek. 'Come on honeybunch,' she said, imitating their father's voice, 'Hope Gardens is on the left.'

Joy looked at her from the corner of her eye, unamused.

Esmine persisted, 'Come on honeybunch, take in the scene.'

Joy couldn't stop herself from smiling.

Esmine smiled in return. Then her face dropped when she noticed the toothless man's eyes on her. 'Come on Joy,' she said, shifting in her seat.

The man lost his balance. 'Take you time no sweet dahta.' He smiled at Esmine.

Joy turned and looked him up and down, 'Excuse me please.'

He stood up and allowed them to pass, holding out his hand to guide Esmine out of her seat.

Esmine looked down at them and squeezed past him.

He wasn't deterred. 'You sweet it's a shame,' he moaned, looking after her.

Joy closed her eyes briefly, certain that the whole bus was looking at them.

'This one for us please,' Esmine said as they forced their way to the front.

'Esmine,' Joy whispered as they got off the minibus, 'at least try not to make yourself sound so English.'

'Oh shut up Joy and come on.' Esmine quickened her pace through the gates of Hope Gardens.

They walked aimlessly through the gardens, drinking skyjuice, discussing trivialties, the real discussion they wanted to have bubbling unspoken beneath the surface.

When they were tired they sat under a mango tree to await their parents, silent, watching Sunday School children from the country walking in line.

Finally Esmine spied them in the distance, 'There they are.' She stood, brushed dried grass from her shorts and legs. 'Let's go Joy.'

They linked arms and walked towards their parents.

Hours later the family were sipping *ting* and snacking on patties in the garden's cafeteria. Esmine swore that mosquitoes were ravishing her body and flies pitching on her lips, and promised that if they didn't go back to Portmore soon she would pass out in the heat.

Joy ignored her, determined to have at least one more pattie, a piece of sweet potato pudding and try another of the many varieties of soft drink on sale. The words she had had with Esmine on the bus had left her feeling uneasy. She looked across at her father. He and her mother were talking and laughing. Esmine was pretending to be reading something or other. *How could she be reading*? Joy thought.

Joy inhaled deeply. The midday heat shimmered off the dusty tarmac. There was a strong smell of soil baked dry by the August heat. She looked up and met her father's eyes. He smiled at her, seeming to be inhaling deeply too. Joy rested back in her chair, a puzzled look in her eyes. Is this what he means? For as long as she could remember he had always told her that when he came back home the sweat of the old people rose in his nostrils. When he used to talk to her about it most of it had seemed so nonsensical.

'I grew up in the country. We had one acre of land,' he would invariably begin. 'It was tough. If you wanted to eat, you had to sweat. Nothing just happened for you. You had to try everything. Planting corn, cultivating yam, growing coffee, whatever you could lay your hands on. But sometimes that wouldn't come to much because the rain didn't fall to help you. So we tried breaking stone, burning coal for houses in town.

'But despite all that, there was something about that piece of land that me pappa passed down to me, and that *his* pappa left for him. The same piece of land that his grandfather buy when he got his freedom from slavery.'

He told Joy that when he used to walk through it after a day's work, there was always a scent that used to make him forget, for a moment, the harshness of his life.

'It used to hit me especially when I passed behind the old house by the family burial plot. It was so strong. At the time I used to think it was me own sweat mixed with the smell of food cooking in people's yards, coffee ripening on the trees, the mangoes I had in my bag, the rotten leaves and the heat baking the land. But when I came to England and went back home for holiday I would smell it. And I didn't have to be in the country, or even near the old land, I could be anywhere in Jamaica.' He would nod forcefully.

Joy would want to tell him it was simple nostalgia, but he would add before she had the chance, 'I'm sure it's just a reminder that my place is still there. Still empty.'

When Joy had come to Jamaica for the first time at thirteen she had not understood. What she had seen then were the luxurious hotels where they had eaten barbecued lobster and jerk chicken. The mangoes, the lizards and the mosquitoes.

She ran her fingers across her lips. Now, at eighteen, despite what her sister thought, she *could* see the stark discrepancy between

7

the rich and the poor. She saw the huge Japanese cars driving past the battered Austin Cambridges. The makeshift restaurants by the roadside and the half-naked children fighting to clean the wind-screen of their own large, air-conditioned hired car.

She saw Parade in downtown Kingston.

In the past week she *had* played the tourist, but now that she could smell the earth she wanted to be its daughter like her father was its son.

'I'm glad we managed to get the fare together for all of us to come out,' Mr Brown was saying. He rubbed the back of his wife's hand. 'It's good for Joy to be here before she goes off to university.' He smiled broadly at his daughter.

Mrs Brown turned to look at him and cleared her throat, 'And Esmine of course needs to rest before she starts her A levels.'

Their father looked sheepishly at his wife.

Joy raised her eyebrow.

Esmine shrugged her shoulders. 'Daddy always forgets me.'

'Esmine, I was about to come round to you when your mother cut in,' he tried to pacify her, 'the two of you have done well . . .'

His wife interrupted. 'We all deserve the rest.' She took her feet out of her sandals and rested them on top of her husband's. 'One thing I know for sure,' she continued, 'my ears needed the rest from the constant nagging.' She looked with a half-smile at Joseph.

He rubbed his hand up and down her back. 'My love, it is three years since we came out here last.' He looked from his wife to Esmine, finally resting his eyes on Joy.

'We should be thankful; some people never manage to get back . . .' Beatrice smiled ruefully.

Joseph picked up his glass and drained it, 'That's them. I couldn't stay more than three years without coming out.' He looked at Joy with a smile, 'What you say about that, Joy?'

Before Joy could answer Esmine jumped in, 'You know Joy is just going to agree with you Daddy . . .'

Her father was irritated by her tone. 'Esmine let Joy speak!'

Beatrice pressed her feet hard into his and cleared her throat, 'I know you tricks you know Joseph. I do not want us to start no big debate on this holiday about where we belong and where we don't belong. You hear me?' She looked from her husband to Joy.

Joy spoke quietly, trying to make sure that her voice didn't show her anger. 'I like the way everyone is trying to silence me. It's not fair . . .'

Esmine tutted, '*Not fair* . . . I hope you're not going to use that one in your law classes at university.'

'Just grow up Esmine.' Joy picked up her glass. 'Go back to your book.' Esmine shrugged, uncaring.

'I never finished what I wanted to say either, dearheart,' Joseph said, smiling at Joy. I agree with you they ganging up on us . . .'

Joy slipped her soursop juice slowly.

'Joseph! You hear what I said?'

'Me love all I was going to say was that I hope this is our last holiday before we all come back for good.'

Esmine raised her eyes to the sky and faked a laugh.

Beatrice sighed, 'You see what I mean? Constant scheming.'

'Not scheming,' Joy said emphatically, 'just planning . . .'

One

Joy sat by the window in the front room, her face buried in her open palms, her eyes narrowed to a slit, watching the steady trickle of rain through the net curtains. South London seemed even more grey and nondescript than it had four weeks ago; the houses drab, secret, unfriendly; the streets devoid of character, empty, quiet, lonely; the sky lost behind layer upon layer of cloud. Not a sound came from outside. Joy couldn't even hear the raindrops.

Esmine's laughter roused her. She was sprawled out on the floor with the phone anchored between her shoulder and her ear, her legs bobbing up and down behind her. She chatted and laughed with one friend after another, making arrangements to meet up, to go out. She had been in that position since the moment they had got in.

Joy got up, cut her eyes at Esmine and left the room.

After dinner, when the family were having tea, Joy plucked up the courage for what she had to say. 'I've decided to go back home,' she said, not looking up from her cup.

Her father gulped, coughed, lowered the mug from his lips to the table, his mouth still open.

'What?' her mother looked at her husband briefly before fixing her eyes on Joy.

'I said I'm going back home!'

Silence.

Esmine laughed, 'What *are* you talking about? You are home . . .'

Joy raised her voice, 'Esmine, shut up!'

Beatrice cleared her throat and creased her forehead. 'Yes! What *are* you talking about? Going home where?'

'Back to Jamaica, of course.'

Her mother fell back in her chair as if pushed. 'What?' She shook her head. 'You must be crazy girl . . .' She looked to her husband for support. He lowered his eyes to the table.

'You really must be crazy!', she repeated emphatically. 'You've got everything here.' She raised her voice. 'You really think I worked my guts out slaving in this place for you to come and tell me nonsense? I gave too much in this country. This is your home, child. You born here. You have a beautiful life here.'

Joy exhaled slowly. She looked directly at her mother. 'Mummy how can I make you understand that living in England makes my life ugly? And I can't do anything about it because if I do, when I do, it always leaves a scar. Like being called filthy dirty names as I go about my business. Like all these years in that *fine* grammar school, frightened stiff, terrified by those constant threats of expulsion when I tried to speak up for myself.' She paused. 'England is leaving too many scars on me.'

'Joy, don't be so melodramatic,' Esmine piped up. 'No place is perfect. There are problems everywhere.'

Joy resisted the temptation to blast her. 'Not the same kind of problems,' she said, pacing her words. 'In Jamaica I can go anywhere, do anything without having to explain, without needing to justify why I exist. I don't have to apologise for being alive.'

'For God's sake don't be so dramatic,' Esmine said.

Joy took a deep breath, 'I really know now that I don't belong here. I can never be happy here. Never!'

Esmine cut her eyes.

Joseph looked down at his hands and sighed.

'Listen girl,' her mother's voice unusually impatient, 'I'm not going to sit here and listen to foolishness.'

'I'm not a child.'

'Joy, watch your tone,' her father said.

Joy flashed him a brief stare, beyond caring. 'Well, I'm not.'

'Joy! I'm not going to tell you again.'

Joy bit her lips.

'The child doesn't seem to be understanding me,' Beatrice said, as if Joy wasn't there. 'Too many of us have had to mash up our families, going here, going there. Like you Uncle Lenford. From Jamaica to England and now him planning to go to America. All that pulling up and moving. For what? I am telling you I for one not doing anymore uprooting and I will not allow my family to split. Not by you Joy or by anybody.'

'Well if you want to stay where you're not wanted . . . I'll just finish my degree, do my articles and then go.'

Joy listened to her mother's relieved sigh. She bit her lips, knowing what was coming, trying hard not to lose her temper.

'By then you would have changed your mind.' Her mother looked at Esmine and smiled. 'Joy, you just come back and you are missing the sun and the sea.'

Joy was furious! 'Mum I'm *not* a shallow child,' she could hear her voice rising and knew her mother would not take kindly to it.

'You could have fooled me,' Esmine piped up.

Joy shot her sister a murderous look, vowing to sort her out later. She turned back to her mother. 'I know what I miss and it's certainly not the sun and the sea. I want us to go back because it is where we belong. Daddy was right all along.'

Her father shifted in his seat and cleared his throat.

Esmine snapped, 'Just speak for yourself, Joy.'

'Esmine, just be quiet!' She looked at her father hoping he would rescue her. He was looking at the palm that he held up to his face.

13

'I want you to stop that kind of talk about belonging in Jamaica . . .'

Joy's voice shook, 'Oh mother. You can talk. You've been here for years and you still talk about *back home*.'

'But that is where I was born. I said already you were born here. You should stay and fight for your right as a British person.'

Joy sighed loudly and tutted as if at her wits end with a particularly dense child.

Her mother spoke firmly, 'Yes! Fight! I . . . We had to fight to get our rightful place here . . . It's *your* birthright! I had to do two jobs for years. Up at the crack of dawn to scrub their stinking dirty toilets, then to the factory to have machines wear down my ear drums. And as if that wasn't enough, I struggled to night school for the piece of paper to get into nursing. I thought then the humiliation would stop. Stop? That was just the beginning. When I was working out my guts to change their old people nasty bedpan and wash their septic sores, they were scorning me, calling me black this and that. I suffered for this place! Now you want to throw it away!' She was exhausted. She fell back in her chair, her fingers pressed on her lips.

Joy didn't care. 'How long do you expect us to go on fighting? Your generation have done all the fighting. They, and generations before that and before that, and where has it got them? What has changed? Nothing! Nothing ever will.' Her voice rose then trailed off.

She looked at her father again, daring him to look at her now. He looked over her head and rubbed his palms across his face and through his hair.

'I know that. I do know that. But it will be different for your generation. Especially with people like you in the ranks. You have your education, your English accents. You use your brains and you are not always saying sorry like we were. I am sorry dear but you just have to face reality. These people won't give without a fight.

There is no running away from that fact.'

Joy sucked her teeth.

'Joy, watch your manners!' Her father's voice was sharp.

She was close to tears. 'I'm sorry,' she snapped, looking at her mother, no less angry than before. 'You didn't stay and fight in Jamaica, did you Mother? Jamaica needed your talents and energy too. But you didn't stay and give them, did you? *You* ran away. Why shouldn't *I* run away too? Why shouldn't we run away? If it was okay then, why isn't it okay now? Daddy, why don't you try and explain to Mummy now?'

Her father looked at her reluctantly. 'Joy you know my feeling and you know your mother do as well . . . You must take things slowly, give everybody a chance to get accustomed to what we . . . you . . . we think is the right thing to do.'

'Your father is right Joy. You musn't push me. I know it is in your nature to be impulsive. I try to understand you. You must at least try to understand me sometimes, and until you do I don't want you to raise this conversation again. You bringing tension and conflict in the family.'

'Yes, Joy,' her father added, 'let's just close the conversation.'

Esmine glared at Joy, 'I don't think this is fair! Joy has been really rude and you are letting her get away with it.' She shifted her accusing gaze to her father, 'You would *never* have put up with it from me.'

'Esmine, please. You heard what your mother said. Let's bring this to an end.'

'No! I think Joy is out of order. She is always causing a division.'

'No I'm not! You don't know what you're talking about.'

'You are trying to divide us. You always do that when it comes to this Jamaica business. You put pressure on Mummy about that wretched place. Why can't you just be content? You should count yourself lucky.'

15

'Now don't you two start carrying on like puss and dog,' Joseph intervened.

'Joy has to be told by somebody since you and Mummy are afraid of her.'

'Oh God!' Joy muttered between clenched teeth.

Esmine continued undeterred, 'I agree with Mummy. You think Jamaica will be all skyjuice . . .'

'Very funny. If you can't say anything more constructive perhaps it's best that you keep your big mouth shut. You've talked enough rubbish for one night.'

'Me! You're the one who's been shouting your mouth off.'

Beatrice slammed her palm on the table, 'I'm fed up with this arguing and fussing. Fed up! Joy, just keep quiet. Why you keep stirring?'

'It's not me. Why are you shouting at me? It's her,' she pointed furiously at her sister.

'*I* didn't bring up the subject. Maybe if you knew when enough is enough. You don't own Jamaica you know.'

'I own more of it than you'll ever own of England. Much more of it.'

'Joy!' her mother bellowed.

Joseph took Beatrice's hand. She snatched it away. 'I've said, shut up your mouth. You have caused enough problem to last me a lifetime. I want you to keep your mouth shut. Now!'

'This is unfair. Why are you shouting at me? You are always blaming me for everything.' Joy leapt up, knocking over her chair.

'Joy, sit down!', her father ordered.

'I'm bloody fed up with the lot of you. Bloody fed up. Just leave me alone!' She rushed from the room, slamming the door behind her.

Joy woke with that sinking feeling of being in disgrace. She waited for her parents to go out before getting up, sighing with relief when Esmine called out that she was going out for the day. Joy didn't want to see her; she would have to make her peace with her later. She was having enough difficulty contemplating facing her mother, and certainly her father. She had gone over the top again. Sworn. Spoken to her mother in a way that even she didn't think was right. She had read her father's eyes, but even that had not stopped her. She spent the day going over how she would make things right with her mother and Esmine. Only her yoga asanas emptied her mind of the turmoil.

Just before she knew her father was due to get home she went for a walk. She needed the air.

He was home when she got back. As soon as she opened the front door he called out to her, 'Joy, is that you?'

'Hello Daddy.' She swallowed, her throat was dry.

She walked slowly into the sitting room.

He was very serious, 'You went out?'

Joy bent and kissed him, 'I went for a walk.'

'Umm . . .' He looked up at her.

'Sit down.' His voice was firm.

Joy's heart sank. She sat next to him, wedging her hands between her legs. He turned to her, his face serious. 'I didn't like the way you behaved last night.'

Joy lowered her eyes and bit her lips.

'Look at me!'

She raised her eyes slowly to meet his.

'You showed no respect for your mother or for me . . .'

'I didn't mean to . . .'

'Joy, listen! You must learn to listen.'

Joy's lips trembled. He had not spoken to her in that tone for a long time.

'I was so ashamed of you last night. I would never have believed I would live to see the day when either of my children,' he lowered his voice, '*especially* you, would speak to their mother like that.' He

17

looked at her, his lips pressed together.

Joy shifted her eyes, she couldn't bear the anger in his eyes.

'I said *look* at me when I'm speaking to you. *Face up to what you have done!*'

Joy bit her lips to stop the tears she knew threatened.

'We brought the both of you up to show respect.' He nodded emphatically as he spoke, his eyes looking fully into his daughter's. 'You mother and me always show one another respect in front of the two of you. And we certainly show you and Esmine respect.' He stopped and waited. 'Is that true or not?'

Joy continued to look at him but couldn't speak.

'Answer me! I asked you a question.'

Joy nodded, her eyes now beginning to water. She had certainly not intended to make him angry. That was the last thing she had wanted. *Oh God he hates me. He's never going to trust me again.* She started to cry.

Her father sighed, 'Joy stop the crying!'

His unsympathetic tone made it worse and she sobbed even more.

He pulled out his handkerchief and gave it to her. He waited, still looking at her, his anger unabated. 'Dry you eyes and calm down. I've always told you crying is no way out of any situation. You *have* to face things.'

Joy managed to get control of herself. She wiped her eyes and blew her nose.

'Right! We have to sort this thing out.' He stopped, then took up again quietly.

Joy could imagine his voice sounding like that when he had broken stones in the heat all day and was now on the brow of the last hill going home. She turned to look at him and regretted her temper and her loose tongue more than ever.

'I have always trusted you because I thought you were always an old head on a young body.' He sighed. 'I know now I was wrong . . .'

18

'Oh Daddy, please don't say that. I *am* sorry . . .'

'It's too late for that now Joy. Just because I have always confided in you about Jamaica doesn't mean I will *ever* allow you to speak out of turn to me or to your mother. You *must* have respect, Joy!'

Joy dropped her shoulders.

'Your mother was very upset by the way you spoke to her last night.'

The pounding in Joy's heart vibrated in her head and made it hurt. The tiredness from her restless night came down on her and the nasty taste in her mouth she had woken with came back again.

As he spoke, each of his words rubbed against the part in her head that was sore. 'I can see why your mother blames me; why she feels I've put you up to it. Why she says that I have been putting you up to it since you were a baby. Why she says that I am scheming with you . . .'

'That's not fair.'

'Joy, you don't seem to hear what I've been saying to you.' He rarely raised his voice and although now it was just above his normal level, it resonated in her ears and she would have cried again if she hadn't been so angry and ashamed at once. So she pressed her big toe into her shoe and into the carpet.

He turned away from her for the first time and stared out through the window. Joy found the silence more painful than his cutting reprimands.

When he turned back to her his face had softened and his voice was back to its characteristic mellowness. 'I do think your mother is right . . .' Joy's big toes moved up and down. She waited but he didn't finish the thought.

'I don't like to see your mother cry, especially when I am the cause of it . . .'

'But you haven't done anything,' her sigh came out broken.

19

His half-smile was sad. 'I have. I have. I have had so many dreams, so many dreams . . .'

Joy wanted to rub the back of his hand but she was afraid he would recoil in anger. All of a sudden she felt extremely lonely. She was about to go off to university . . . Her mother was angry with her . . . Her father was both angry *and* disappointed and would never trust her again, and her sister thought she was stupid.

She pressed the palm of her hand on her face, more depressed than she had been for years. It had all backfired on her. This was not how she thought it would be when she made the decision to go back home. This was not how her father had led her to believe it would be. *I should be the one who's angry, not him. He's the one who started this whole hunger in me and now he's just left me to face the heat by myself.*

Joy felt a great bitterness rise in her. If she thought she could get away with it she would tell him all that and then stomp out of the room. She knew better, and she stayed, controlling herself.

When he spoke again Joy regretted her secret anger. 'From the time I saw you, my first child, slide into the world, for some reason I imagined that my dreams would be your dreams too. For the life of me I have not been able to explain why. But now I know that your mother is right . . .'

'Daddy they *are* my dreams.'

He looked at her and shook his head.

'There has been no greater joy in the world for me than seeing you and Esmine grow up and succeed, despite this wretched and God-forsaken country.' He sighed, 'It's been like planting seed in a ground that I know is barren, a ground that chokes and kills most kinds of seed, and seeing them not just grow but flourish . . .'

He tried to smile but only one side of his mouth went up. Instead, he cocked his head to one side and looked at her. 'Look Joy, all I ever wanted is for you and your sister to know that you are not rootless. You come from somewhere. You *belong* somewhere . . .'

Joy nodded. 'Daddy please let me say something.'

He looked at her for a moment before speaking. 'Okay, I suppose I've had my say. So long as you are sure you understand me. I won't tolerate disrespect. You are never too old . . .' He stopped.

Joy sighed, feeling more wretched than before. 'I do understand. I am sorry for last night, I will apologise to Mummy.'

He nodded. 'Good. So what you want to say now?'

Joy cleared her throat, 'I know I was out of order last night, but Daddy I do *really* understand it now.' Her eyes widened as she held his eye. He sat up, his whole body relaxed towards her.

'That day in Hope Gardens, I saw the heat making patterns above the ground. I smelt it that day Daddy. And I saw what you meant about how you and my grandparents have worked to make a place for us there.' Joy nodded as if to emphasise her words.

Her father's face was a parcel of victory and caution.

Joy pressed her advantage, 'I knew you smelt it too that day because I *saw* it in your eyes.' She stopped, as he would have done to allow her words to sink in. 'It was then that I knew that you had always been right.'

He rested back in his chair and Joy knew he had finally conquered the hill, walked down the gully and got home. He had put his bag down, and was sitting on the bench in the yard, drinking sugar'n water. His eyes had lit up and he smiled. He nodded repeatedly, his whole body shaking, seeming to forget his anger of a moment ago. 'I thought you did. I thought you did. The old people never let me down.' Then, with a seriousness replacing his glee, 'Your mother won't want to hear that Joy. She will say it's foolishness.'

Joy sighed, the only hint of a criticism of her mother she knew she would be permitted in his presence.

He rubbed his hand over his head. 'We have to take it slowly Joy. I want you to understand, honeybunch.'

Joy smiled at the use of her pet name. Perhaps he didn't hate her

21

after all. She spoke softly, ready to stop at the slightest sign of disapproval. 'How slowly? Suppose Mummy is never ready. Suppose she never wants to go back? What are we . . . you going to do?'

He ran his thumb across his chin. 'Give her time Joy. I have waited for all these years. I understand her. I can still wait. She will come round. I know she will. Eventually.'

Joy raised her eyebrow when he looked away from her.

'Your mother will want you and Esmine to go to college and finish first, then we can raise it again . . . After all . . .' his voice became distant, 'I didn't want to come here in the first place but I didn't want to lose her so I squeezed me toes and came. Against my better judgments I came.' He shook his head. 'Through thick and thin I stayed. Through the ill treatment, the insults and the bad life.

'So she owes it to me, to us, to go back when the time comes. I hope to God she will come round. It will be the greatest tragedy for me if she doesn't come round.' He shook his head and left his words to hang in the room.

He turned to look at Joy then. His eyes were red. She thought for an awful moment he would cry. The only time she had seen him do that was when the telegram had come to say that his mother had died. He had not been there, not to talk about her at the Set Up and to sing at the Nine Night.

Joy moved a little closer to him and waited. She didn't know what to say. If she hadn't just been told off by him, if last night hadn't happened, she would have been her normal self, relaxed and at ease with the father she adored. Now she didn't know what he wanted. She didn't know what to say.

It was a long time before he spoke again. 'So until this breath leaves this body I will try to turn your mother round and I pray and hope that all four of us, but if not all four of us – for after all you and Esmine were born here –' he saw Joy's frown but continued, 'if not all four of us, I pray with all my heart that your mother and I will go back. I owe it to the old people . . .' His eyes became distant again.

'Daddy, you must believe that I want to go back too; that I have to go back as well.' She looked deeply in his eyes to be convinced that he believed. She couldn't tell. Her depression deepened.

She looked away from him, remembering the days when he had coached her through the pains of school. The days when she had sat with Esmine and listened to him, boasting of his life in St John's Road, St Catherine, exhorting them to higher things.

'Let me tell you sweethearts,' he would say, 'you have to be twice as good as those white girls you call your friends before you get anywhere. Don't ever forget it or let anyone fool you. None of these white people are going to do you any favours. You better learn to stand on your own two feet.'

They would be in the dining room, their mother knitting and looking up occasionally to meet his eyes, and smile at Esmine and then at Joy.

'Do you lessons in school and ignore all the distractions, like some of those half-dead boys you see hanging around the place. Don't either of you even *think* of bringing one of them in this house. You hear me?' He would wait for some reaction before continuing.

Joy was always the one to raise her eyebrow and reply, 'Yes Daddy.' Then she would exchange glances with Esmine.

'Education is the only thing we can see you get before we leave this place . . .'

Hardly a Saturday had passed when he did not bring up the subject of *worthless* boys and his favourite topic, education. 'First of all, white people say A, think B . . . especially if they are talking about black people.' He would shake his finger in their direction. 'Mind, I'm not telling you to not have respect for you teachers. But what you have to remember is that they too have been believing lies for years . . . they too have been lied to and so most of

23

them don't know A from bullfoot when it comes to black people . . .'

That was one of Joy's favourite little sayings of his from back home.

'Whatever they say though, you girls must learn to pick the good out from the bad, you hear me?' His voice strong, as if exemplifying the strength he knew they would need.

'Later on you won't be able to tell the colleges that you failed your exams because of teachers. They will just laugh in your face. As for all this complaining about what this and that girl call you, just let it wash over you. Words can't do very much . . . Walk far from trouble. A warning you . . .'

He was always so strong, so certain that whatever Joy and Esmine had to face, they would make it in the end.

Not for one moment, in those days, did Joy think he ever waivered. When people asked her who she most admired in the whole world or who she wanted to be like when she grew up, she had always said, 'My father of course.'

'Your mother will be home soon.' Joseph got up and stretched.

'Daddy,' Joy looked up at him. 'I *am* sorry . . .'

'I do hope you understand honeybunch,' he bent and kissed her on the top of her head. 'What you say? Your law degree will take three years and the book you gave me said two years for the . . .?'

'Articles.'

'Ummm. So that's five years.'

Joy nodded.

'We'll be patient until then. Your sister will have finished at the art college she says she wants to go to.' He smiled broadly. 'Then we can bring up the subject again. By then Beatrice should be ready to go back. By then, she will be on our side.' He stopped and thought. 'By then there will be no more excuses to make . . .'

The optimistic look on his face raised Joy's spirit for the first time since they had returned from holiday. She jumped up and hugged him, really ready now to face her mother.

Two

At first the freedom was intoxicating. But it wasn't long before Janet was plagued with guilt.

She had defied her father and left Birmingham to attend art college in London. She didn't know how she had found the strength to stand up to him, her father, the founder and overseer of the Church of the Brethren Called from Darkness, pastor of the biggest branch.

For as long as Janet could remember she had been burdened by it. Her life up to leaving had been anything but normal. She had never been like other people she had known at school. Her life was school, home, church. The latter three or four times a week. Sleep. School. Home. Church. The pattern rarely varied.

Saturdays she shopped with her mother; cleaned the house; polished the furniture; emptied the cupboards, the wardrobes, the drawers in her room. Hoovering, cooking, television, studying, sleep. Sunday morning family worship, church . . .

She had been saved when she was eight. Before that, she had read the Bible from cover to cover, had been baptised and filled with the Holy Ghost.

She remembered little of the soul-searching sermons, revival meetings and dancing in the spirit down the aisles. What she did know was that they couldn't have changed much. *God never changes, so nothing else should ever change*. She remembered hearing *that* constantly.

What she remembered too was that she was afraid all the time. All the stories and admonitions about goodness and light, and badness and darkness, and damnations, and the threat of hell fire never left her.

Life was always such a *burden* for her. She felt the eyes of the maker on her constantly. *And the adversary, the devil, as a roaring lion*, sought to devour her, constantly reminding her that on the scales of good and evil she weighed heavily in favour of evil.

She tried to change, would search herself constantly, fast and pray, but she was still a worthless sinner destined to be damned.

She remembered Dives and Lazarus. She could only have been four or five when she first heard the story in Sunday School. Dives was in hell, burning night and day, burning constantly but couldn't die. He was always thirsty. He had been bad when he was alive. He had died but was alive again. Strange, she had thought.

Lazarus had been poor but good. He had also died but was alive again. Dives could see Lazarus on the other side. In heaven.

Dives saw Lazarus and remembered that he had not helped Lazarus in their other life, and now he was dying of thirst but couldn't die. So he begged Lazarus to give him a drink. Even a drip from his finger would have done. But Lazarus couldn't help him because there was a gulf between them. Dives had to suffer in hell. Thirsty. Burning. Forever. Never dying.

At eight years old, Janet had found it all hard to imagine but had decided that it must have been the most awful thing ever.

She had thought about it so much that she had started to dream about it. First she was Lazarus. But that was horrible because she hated to see Dives burning in hell. Then she was Dives and Lazarus would not help her and she was thirsty, burning and never dying.

She tried to blot it out. The constant vision of hell and burning and thirst. She prayed and gave to the church, visited the sick, the unsaved, the backsliders. She was a good Christian. Her father made certain of that: 'My children have to be an example. How can I lead spiritual children unless my own are perfect?'

The escape to London was a desperate attempt to lose sight of hell, burning and thirst.

London was so different. There were few reminders of her evil ways. It was like breathing pure fresh air. But to appease her father she kept her promise to go home every weekend in her first two terms and she testified with great feeling of her victories over Satan. She vowed to packed congregations that she was going to hold on to the end whatever happened. The amens rang out loud and clear.

But at home after services her father did not let up. He reminded her that he was not a fool. She *had* ignored his wishes and gone to London, and she would have to give an account to God for her disobedience.

The first day her father surprised her in London she had been alone in the flat she shared with two other girls. It was the second term of her first year.

It had been a Wednesday evening and so rest night from church. The rap on the door startled her. She had not been expecting anyone.

She left the design she had been sketching for her portfolio and answered the door.

When she saw her father she nearly collapsed. Her room was in a mess.

'Daddy! What are you doing here? Is anything wrong?'

He stepped past her into the hall. 'Do I need to give a reason to visit you?'

'No, but . . .'

'I trust you are not going to keep me standing here in the hallway?' His voice was impatient, his expression set.

27

'No,' Janet turned and led him up to her room. She could hear her heart pounding. Just being near him always did that to her.

As she climbed the stairs she sifted through her mind for a reason for his sudden appearance. She had sent her tithes from her grant at the beginning of the term. She had written last week. She had phoned last night.

She walked tentatively into her room and turned to see his scornful eyes surveying it. He made a scraping noise in his throat as if trying to dislodge mucus. 'I see why you don't want to let me in. This room is a mess! It hasn't taken you long to forget your home training. Have you forgotten that cleanliness is next to Godliness?'

She looked from him to the room, 'Daddy, I'm working . . .'

'You can't be working with materials, books and records at the same time.' He bent and picked up one of the albums.

Janet felt sick and faint.

'What kind of record is this?' He turned the album over, 'This is certainly not a spiritual record.'

The dreadlocks on the sleeve of the album were blurred. Janet tried to focus on them but they came and went, like the rest of the room.

'Don't you hear I'm speaking to you?' He shook the album in front of her before dropping it on the floor.

Janet looked down at it.

He started to shout, 'The Lord knows why He revealed to me to come down here this evening.'

She sat down, fearing she would tumble if she didn't. She did not know then that she would be sitting in that position for the next three hours.

He flung his briefcase on the floor, snapped it open, took out his Bible and another one for her. 'God knows if you remembered to bring yours down.' Janet glanced across the room to see hers on the bedside table. Why has he noticed everything else and not that? Obediently she took the one he handed her.

He stood over her, a mountain of fury, his eyes bulging red. 'You see all those fiery testimonies you giving when you come up at weekends? I'm not fooled by them. I have the spirit. You hear me?' He jabbed the air with pointed fingers. 'You cannot hide from God! His watchful eyes are on you, following you wherever you go. I beg you to remember that.' He shook his oversized Bible in her face.

Janet squeezed back into the chair.

'Open you Bible!'

She obeyed, her hands shaking violently, not sure which of the pages to rest on.

'I said open and read,' he shouted, pacing the room, his own Bible aloft.

The Bible opened to St John 3:16.

'For God so loved . . .' Janet croaked.

'Loved . . . Loved . . .!' he thundered, thumping the side of his thigh, 'You lucky God is not like man.' He ordered her to find another and another until she found ones he wanted, ones painting graphic pictures of hell and despair.

'Where the worms die not and the fire is never quench . . .' Tears burnt their way down her cheeks as she read.

'The Lord is dealing with you! Turn to another . . . Read up.'

'. . . I will bring distress . . . their blood shall be poured out like dust, and their flesh like dung . . .'

'Find another. Let the Lord do his work on you.'

'. . . and he shall be tormented with fire and brimstone . . .'

And so it went on, and on, and on.

That visit was the beginning.

She would never be sure when he would come. If she was out he would wait in his car or if one of her flatmates were in, in the sitting room, reading his Bible until she came. Then the two of them would have a prayer meeting. She would make excuses for her friends, despite his insistence that they should be there, cringing with discomfort as his voice rose and fell, exhorting her and praying for her and for them.

Those meetings weakened Janet's resolve, and she would have given in and gone back home to Birmingham had she not met Esmine.

She had seen her around the college. Esmine stood out. She was very tall and slim, skin dark and smooth, accentuating her big brown eyes. A thick head of hair, cut in style, the back resting on her shoulders, the front shorter and more curly. And her walk. Upright. Long strides, her feet, it seemed never quite touching the ground. Her neck long, her head thrown back. She had so many friends, was always with somebody, always had people watching her.

Janet watched her too, overawed by her confidence and beauty. It didn't seem to bother Esmine that she was one of just a handful of black students in the college. Janet would have gone through college not daring to speak to her had Esmine not introduced herself.

Esmine had joined her in a bank queue just outside the college. She didn't hesitate, 'Hi. I'm Esmine. I've seen you around college.' She extended her hand, long manicured nails, a single silver ring on her index finger.

Janet smiled, looking behind her briefly to see if Esmine was addressing someone else.

'You're Janet aren't you?'

Janet nodded and took her hand. It was soft.

'I hate waiting in queues, don't you?'

She didn't want to sound foolish. 'Yes,' was all she managed.

Her muteness didn't deter Esmine. She moved next to her and chatted until Janet's turn came.

'Let's go for coffee afterwards,' she suggested as Janet moved off to the counter.

'Okay.'

As Janet took her money from the cashier she cringed. She had managed only two words throughout their entire conversation.

But the coffee was fun. Esmine was lively and friendly, more interested in telling Janet about her classes, her family and her friends, than worrying about Janet's silence. And as time went on they became friends, Janet charmed by Esmine's vivacity, Esmine finding strength in Janet's quiet calm.

Janet often stayed at Esmine's home, knew her parents and had met Joy a couple of times when she had come home from university for the weekend. She burned to tell Esmine about the problems in her own family but felt sure that from the cocoon of her own warm home Esmine would never understand. She envied Esmine her parents and her sister.

One weekend after Joy had visited, Janet told Esmine, 'You are so lucky . . . You are so close . . .'

Esmine pursed her lips, 'Don't be fooled, it's not as rosy as you think . . .'

'It looks like that to me.'

Esmine sighed, 'If you really want to know, I'm dreading Joy coming back from university.'

'You joking. Why?'

'Don't get me wrong. I adore her . . .' Esmine shook her head and stretched out on the floor beside Janet. '. . . She's everything I've ever wanted to be . . .'

'What? I don't believe that.'

'I've never admitted it to anyone.'

Janet sat up and looked down at her friend. 'I don't understand why.'

'Oh, lots of reasons. She knows what she wants; she's strong . . . She doesn't care what anybody thinks of her.' Esmine rolled over on her back, 'And she's Daddy's favourite . . .'

'Never . . . Your father is so . . . so human. He seems to adore both of you.'

31

Esmine rubbed her fingers across her lips, 'No, he's always loved her best. She's never disappointed him . . .'

'In what? You're doing well too . . .'

'Not as well as Joy. She graduates at the end of this term in law . . . I'm just at art college. Daddy doesn't rate that.'

Janet watched her friend, wanting to tell her how small all that seemed compared with what she had to face.

Esmine stood up and faced the mirror, running her fingers across her forehead and down her cheeks. 'I suppose what I'm dreading more than anything is that Joy is going to come back and start up a long-running thing that's been going on in our family for as long as I can remember.'

'What's that?'

Esmine sat on the side of the bed. 'She's obsessed with the idea of emigrating to Jamaica.'

Janet frowned. 'Jamaica! Why?'

Esmine shook her head. 'God knows. She's always going on about it being home and all that. Daddy planted all that in her head.'

'I would never have thought there was any similarity between your dad and mine . . .'

'Umm?'

'Heavenly home . . . The celestial city. That's my dad's obsession, making it into the heavenly home.'

Esmine looked at Janet, puzzled.

Janet got up and sat on a chair, facing her, 'At least there is no real pressure on you. My dad puts so much pressure on me,' and she went on to tell Esmine about her father's visits.

'You joking! Why didn't you tell me? How long's this been going on?'

'Since last term.'

'God.'

'I feel so caved in. So trapped. There is nothing I can do to stop him and yet I can't stand it. It's cracking me up.'

'It's bizarre! What about your mother? Why don't you talk to her?'

'Poor Mum.'

'What do you mean?'

'She wouldn't want to go against him, and besides, she wouldn't see what harm it's doing . . . She'd say it's because he cares.'

Esmine was emphatic, 'Do something about it yourself then.'

'What can I do?'

'Well, start with excuses for not going home every weekend. Go once a month or even less. Say it's to do with college. Tell him that you have evening lectures and pin him down to an exact time when he should visit for the prayer meetings. Say you've found a church in London to go to, and learn to act,' Esmine smiled.

'What?'

'When you go home let him think you're totally engrossed. When he comes, invite a few of us to the meeting and he'll think you're really being a good example to us.'

Janet wasn't sure, but she went along with Esmine's ideas. At first it seemed to work. She knew when he would come and there were always four of five of them waiting. It pleased him beyond measure.

When she went home he beamed at her from the pulpit and made her the subject of a number of his sermons '. . . Janet comes back home full of the power and the glory of the Lord! I thought she was slipping, but after much prayer and fasting for her, the Lord touched her. *Glory to the Lord*! And now her burning desire for the Lord has come back. Oh yes! God has touched the dry bones in the valley and flesh has come unto it again . . .' He shouted and danced around the rostrum in triumph.

Janet sank in her seat.

'. . . Oh yes brethren, as Ezekiel wrote, I said I will not speak any more in his name but his words were in me like burning fire shut up in my bones and I could not stay . . .'

There was much rejoicing for her.

Back in London the guilt of her deception weighed heavily, and she waited for the hand of God to strike her down.

But the more the vision of His hand threatened her the more she found *pleasures of the world* to suppress the vision and the guilt.

The long summer holiday that she had to spend in Birmingham left her pining for the Blues Esmine had introduced her to.

Those parties with throbbing bodies and pounding music had been strange at first. She felt like a fish out of water, but then it all came together. Was it Bob Marley's 'No Woman No Cry'? or Culture's 'When the Two Seven Clash' that signalled the release of a different fire within her? Wordly pleasures? Had she *backslid* from the heavenly path to become a sinner again?

As she sat in the congregation shouting and rejoicing to gospel choruses she dreamt of nights in London when she would dance to a different tune. She would look at her father and wonder what he'd do if he knew of her indulgence in the sins of the flesh.

She suppressed the periods of intense guilt at first with great difficulty and then with increasing ease. The prayer meetings in her room continued for the next two years and she gloated at her secret victory over her father's spirit of discerning.

But one evening, after a particularly fervent prayer meeting, Janet noticed that her keys were gone. The other four women who had stayed with her for the meeting emptied their bags but the keys were nowhere to be found. She wondered whether her father had picked them up by mistake.

When she called him later to ask he did not give her a straight answer. She thought it strange but knew it was his way to turn the simplest question into a maze.

It was not long before she found out that he had taken her keys. Previously he had made his surprise visits alone, but that night he came with her mother.

Janet was not alone – Roger was there. She had not known him long but things had moved along rather quickly. They were listening to an album and sitting on the sofa with their backs to the door. The only light came from a lamp by her bed. Anyone coming into the room would be fooled into thinking that it was empty but for the intermittent giggles coming from the sofa.

Janet had not heard them come in.

The first she heard was her father's voice. 'She's not here.'

Janet and Roger sprang up simultaneously.

'Who the hell are you?' Roger shouted, taking a step towards them.

Janet opened her mouth to stop him but no sound came out. She couldn't look at her mother. The shock on her father's face held her eyes.

'I said who the hell are you? How did you get in?' Getting no reply, he turned to Janet, 'Jan I thought you locked the door?'

She had still not managed to close her mouth.

He looked back to the strangers, back to her and then again to them.

Janet's mother whispered, 'Jesus have mercy.'

Janet found her voice. It came like sandpaper against metal, 'Roger, please go. My parents . . .'

She caught the look of confusion on his face as he scrambled for his shoes.

It was as if she was suspended on the ceiling watching it all, and for a split second she wanted to hold her stomach and laugh. Then she remembered that she was one of the players in the game, not a mere spectator.

She slid back on to the settee as Roger slammed the bedroom door.

As they came round to face her all the energy drained from her.

It was her father who unleashed. 'You are a loose and disgusting child . . . You have committed yourself . . . You are nasty and disgusting . . .'

That was just the beginning. Like a caged animal he paced the room, sweating, shouting, preaching.

She sat for what seemed like hours, listening, but wishing that she could blot out his words, her heart bursting, tears stinging her eyes and face. With mounting anger she listened, humiliated, driven back to her childhood, when she had no power to question.

Her mother said nothing, just sat and wrung her hands.

'You will pack up now. You will leave the course! Tonight. Come back with us, before you become a total disgrace . . . before you are totally lost . . . kneel down you sinful child . . . Come!' He motioned to his wife, 'let us lay hands on her.'

She got up and stood with her husband over Janet, her hand resting on her daughter's shoulder.

Her father's hand came down on her head. He grasped a handful of hair. Janet winced and moved to loosen his grip. Tears seeped from her eyes. His hand dug deeper into her hair; his grasp tightened as he moved his hand around. Strands of her hair came away from the scalp. His prayer resounded in her ears and her neck and face were sprayed with his thick saliva. Janet remained on her knees until her head and shoulders were bruised and she was tired and lifeless from their laying on of hands.

Then, without warning, he strutted across the room, throwing aside or kicking anything that was remotely in his way. Her small table crashed, sending her music centre, records and tapes flying. Her tapes were trampled underfoot, records pulled from their sleeves and broken before being flung on the floor. Her portfolio, neatly set by the side of her bed was picked up by his right foot, scattering fabric samples, drawings, sketches around the room. At her wardrobe he swung open the door and started to pull clothes out and on to the floor.

'Get up and pack. Now! You are going back with us . . .'

Clothes that didn't come readily off the hangers were ripped, the hangers broken.

Janet's mouth dropped. She looked across to her mother for help, but she only shook her head and did not move to intervene.

Janet didn't know what got into her then. She jumped up, rushed to where he was and stood in front of him. It had only occurred to her then that she could never go back home. 'I'm not going back.'

'Say what?' he screamed, beside himself, perspiration dripping down the side of his contorted face.

Janet was shaking. 'I said I'm not going back.' She held his eyes, something she had not dared to do before.

He turned to his wife briefly then flashed furious eyes at his daughter. 'You dare to disobey me. You dare!'

Janet knew she had taken him off guard. 'Leave my clothes alone and get out of my room.' She grabbed a pair of trousers he had just taken out.

'Janet.' It was her mother. She walked like someone burdened down with an unbearably heavy load. She stood next to her husband, her eyes on Janet. 'What has come over you? You have never spoken to your father like this before.' Her mother's voice hardly carried to her, although they could almost have rubbed noses.

Janet hugged the trousers she was holding. 'Well tell him Mummy. He can't throw my clothes on the floor. He can't order me to go home . . . he can't . . . I haven't done anything . . . And . . . And I'm in the middle of my finals . . .'

Her father's brow creased and his face became like the clouds threatening a storm.

Janet's mother looked to him but he could not have seen her. He reached out to grab Janet, but she pushed his hand away and stepped back, turned, ran across the room and threw open her door. 'Get out!'

37

'This child is possessed by the devil,' he turned to his wife, his lips trembling.

'I'm nearly twenty-one. I am not a child. You shouldn't have taken my keys. You are a liar. A liar!' The tears came then and, almost as if at the same moment, her flatmates appeared, concerned about the noise.

'Shut the door. Now! I order you to shut the door.' He walked across to her.

Janet put herself in front of the opened door. 'I said go. I will not shut the door until you get out of my room.'

He stopped and looked back at his wife. 'The child is possessed . . .'

Janet's mother walked across the room and held him by the elbow, 'Dear. This is ungodly . . . It is getting out of hand.'

He looked vacantly at her and then back at Janet. 'I am giving you the last chance to do as you are told. I said *shut* the door . . .'

'No! *I said get out!* This is my room.'

Janet's flatmates were whispering. One of them asked, 'Janet, is everything all right?'

She screamed at them, 'Just go away!'

They hesitated and then crept back into the sitting room.

Janet's mother sighed and tugged at her husband's elbow. He allowed himself to be led to where he had deposited his briefcase. She picked it up and gave it to him, took up her own bag and led him back to the door.

He stepped past Janet without looking at her.

It was her mother who spoke, 'Janet. You know it is not right to dishonour your parents . . . Your pastor.'

'Mummy I just want him to get out of my room . . .'

Janet stepped back and made to slam the door.

He moved quickly and put his foot in front. 'You will hear me out . . . There will be no place in my house for you until you repent. Believe me girl, dishonouring your parents is a sin.' He stepped forward, snarling, his eyes flashing red with fury, 'It would be better if a millstone were hung around your neck and you were drowned.'

'You shouldn't be saying that. I haven't done anything for you to put that kind of curse on me,' Janet said hysterically.

He looked her up and down. 'Curse? *I* am not the devil worshipper. Nothing beats prayer my girl! The God of Heaven is not dead.' He raised his finger and pointed at her, 'Let me tell you one thing. He will teach you to dishonour me. I will be alive to see Him rest his hands on you for your behaviour tonight.' He nodded and pointed up, 'I will be alive . . . Vengence is the Lord's. He will repay you!'

'Daddy that's terrible! You're wrong to call vengence on me. You shouldn't . . . shouldn't . . .'

But he turned sharply and strutted down the steps. His wife behind him.

Janet slammed the door after them.

Janet was unable to get his words out of her mind. She tried to dismiss them, even to laugh at the response she had made to them. She told herself that nothing he said could affect or hurt her. But the words lingered in her mind and the passing weeks and months did not lessen their impact.

She had barely finished her course when the nightmares began. She was in an enclosed place; a lift or the tube. And someone would turn to look at her. She shifted in discomfort. Then she realised that *everyone* there was looking at her. She felt her panic rise. One man leaned forward, arms outstretched. She gasped and leaned backwards but his hands were reaching for her throat and he was muttering, the words getting louder and louder: *Honour thy father and thy mother that thy days may be long upon the earth . . . Whoso shall offend one of these little ones which believe in me, it were better for him that a millstone were hanged about his neck and that he were drowned . . .*

Try as she might, she couldn't move out of his way. She tried to scream, to run, to beg for mercy, to ask forgiveness, but no words came and she knew she was doomed.

She graduated from college and found herself exiled in London. She was afraid to call home and she was afraid not to call, so in the end she resigned herself to a new life without her parents. But the prospect of such stark and unfamiliar isolation frightened and confused her.

Then, one day, on her way to work, she heard someone call her name. She looked back, the road was empty. She heard her name again, recognising the voice. She stopped. The voice was not coming from behind her but from above. She started to run, petrified. The voice followed her, becoming louder and more piercing, calling her, reciting . . .

Honour thy father and thy mother that thy days may be long upon the earth . . . Whoso shall offend one of these little ones which believe in me, it were better for him that a millstone were hanged about his neck and that he were drowned . . .

She felt she needed her parents then.

She needed their prayers, but how could she ask them for prayer when she had so dishonoured them?

Three

It was only afterwards that Joy realised her mother *must* have had a premonition of her death.

Looking back she could see all the tell-tale signs that in the bustle and action she had overlooked.

Now, the memory of that last week was so strong in Joy's mind that she could conjure it up at will. She remembered little of the resentment she had felt towards her mother, only a happy domestic scene; the four of them sitting around the dining table, laughing and talking, Joy and her father on one side, her sister and their mother facing them.

Her mother had taken a week off work. That in itself was unusual. For as long as Joy could remember her parents had synchronised their holidays. They were fresh from Esmine's graduation.

Beatrice looked briefly at Joy, 'You girls have been working so hard for so long with one exam or another that we hardly see each other.' Her eyes lingered on her youngest daughter. 'Now that you have finished college we can have more time together.'

She fixed her eyes on Joy, 'I want us to really be together this week. I want us all to spend some time together, okay?'

Joy smiled and nodded.

Beatrice lowered her eyes to her plate, shifting her food around but raising nothing to her lips.

Joy watched her mother closely. She had noticed that she was not her usual self but thought it was because she and Esmine had finished their studies, *were now going to be working women*, as she put it.

Now Joy wondered whether it was because the time had come to reopen the topic that had been closed for some time.

Nobody had brought it up, but there was a change in her mother's walk, in the way she spoke, in her eyes.

Joy glanced at Esmine. She too was picking at her fish. Joseph looked up. He was serious. 'Bea, how you voice sound so? You tired you know.'

Beatrice raised her eyes slowly from her plate, met his eyes but didn't answer.

Joy's skin prickled in the silence. She rubbed her arm and felt goose pimples. It wasn't cold. It was unusually mild for the time of year.

She heard Esmine's sigh. 'Yes Mummy I've been thinking that you do look kind of . . . I don't know, not exactly if tired . . .?'

'Vacant . . . as if you are somewhere else . . .'

'Thank you Joy,' Esmine said, 'finishing off my sentence for me as usual.' She gave one of her slanted smiles.

'Sorry my darling sis. Anyway that's not true. I don't usually do that . . . do I?'

Esmine blew her a kiss across the table and nodded.

Joy shrugged. '*Are* you all right Mummy?'

'Of course I am dear.' But she shook her head slowly, and even that familiar gesture was somehow different.

Joseph grunted but his wife got in first, 'Joseph please don't start any of you, *I know you like I know myself* nonsense now. I am not tired. I am not vacant, I am not anywhere else. I just want to spend some time with you and me children.'

She tried to smile at him but her lips trembled, 'Just pass the pepper sauce please and stop trying to peer into me soul.'

She took the bottle and turned the red seeded liquid over her fish

42

and rice. Then she turned brightly to her husband. 'Jo honey, the girls have done us proud eh?' She knew that would straighten him up.

It worked. He turned to Joy, smiled broadly at her and picked her hand off the table. He glanced across at Esmine but turned back to Joy, the light in his eyes growing brighter as he spoke.

'Yes me dear. All the heartache and the pain and the tears was worth it . . . *We have a solicitor in our house . . .*'

Beatrice cleared her throat.

Joy wanted to pull her hand away, embarrassed, but it was too late . . . 'And an interior designer,' he added.

The light faded as he smiled across at his youngest daughter.

Esmine pouted her painted lips, 'Daddy doesn't rate designers.'

'Dear, of course I do . . .'

'That is not what you implied the other day Daddy.'

Joy pressed her lips together. She didn't like the tone Esmine was using to her father. 'Esmine don't start that again.'

'Joy, just be quiet. I wasn't talking to you. And anyway you weren't there.' She cut her eyes at Joy and looked first at her mother and then back to her father. Her bottom lip was trembling. She sounded hurt. 'Daddy said I should have done another degree like history. And that wasn't the first time. Ever since I decided to do art you have been saying that I should have chosen something else.' Esmine looked to her mother for support.

Beatrice looked down at her plate.

Joy stretched out her legs and bit her lips. She couldn't believe Esmine. Tonight of all nights. Couldn't she see that something was wrong with their mother and that she shouldn't be causing upset?

She raised her voice. 'For God's sake Esmine, when are you going to stop being so sensitive?'

'Joy please don't raise your voice at the table.' Her mother's eyes widened. She turned to rub the back of Esmine's hand.

Joseph tried to appease her, 'Esmine you mustn't make it sound like that. I was only meaning that if we go home . . .'

Beatrice tutted and glared at him.

He wasn't looking at her, '. . . you may find it hard to get fixed up with a job.'

'Joseph! Not now!' She got up and started clearing the table.

He continued trying to apologise. 'I was only going to say, Bea, that Esmine mustn't upset herself so. I am proud of both of them the same, love both of them the same . . .' He looked down and realised that he was still holding Joy's hand. He gently pulled his hand away.

Joy rubbed the hand he had been holding. It was warm. She too had forgotten he had it. His hand had felt so much like an extension of her own.

Joseph sighed. 'So you were saying Bea, you want us to do something together this week?'

Joy was glad that his voice was back to normal.

But her mother's was not, and neither were her eyes. They seemed far away and cloudy. 'Not just *do* something. I want us to be together.'

Joseph swallowed and nodded.

'Joy, I hope you hear what Mummy is asking.' Esmine put her elbow on the table and rested her chin in her palm.

Joy sighed loudly. 'Of course. Why do you need to say that?' Joy did not hide the irritation in her voice but she was careful not to shout, as she felt like doing.

'Just to make sure you tell that boyfriend of yours that you can't be with him this week. That you are going to spend some time with us.'

Joy raised her eyebrow. 'For your information Esmine I do *not* spend all my time with Lee . . .'

'*You do*! Despite all the pretence about being in control of the relationship and not wanting a long-term commitment. You've been saying that for nearly five years. Before long Joy will be walking up the aisle.'

44

'Don't be so stupid Esmine. You don't know anything about our relationship.'

'I know enough! You are such a hypocrite. All the talk about being an independent career woman. You are a joke.'

Joy was furious. She looked at her mother and then at her father but they were exchanging amused glances.

Joseph looked up at them, 'Puss and dog! Puss and dog!' he grinned.

So although it was a Saturday and Joy had promised Lee to spend the night at his place, she stayed at home, talking with her family and trying hard not to rile her sister.

But late in the night she felt a nagging unease. She could not work out what had come over her mother. She had never seen her like this before. Perhaps, it was the coming of the dark early nights, the leaves turning brown, falling and rotting. Perhaps it was beginning to depress her mother too. Eventually she fell asleep, unease still gnawing at her stomach.

In the morning she heard her parents talking as she passed their room, but their tones were subdued, her mother's voice unplayful, serious, emphatic. Joy sighed, imagining her mother telling her father to, 'stop carrying on as if you only have one child.'

Joseph sat on the edge of the bed, watching her.

'Bea, you know that is not fair. You know that I love both girls the same.'

She glared at him, 'You know it's me you talking to and you can't tell me nonsense. You never make the effort to really talk to Esmine. It's as if she is just not there.'

'Honey, you know I don't do it purposely . . .'

He reached out to hold her arm. She took a step back.

'Don't honey me. It must hurt Esmine.' She pulled her dress forcefully over her head and turned for him to zip her up.

He stood up, kissed her on the neck, and bent, planting kisses as far down her spine as the opened zip would allow.

She smiled, amazed that even after twenty-five years the mere touch of his lips still sent a cold tingle down her spine.

'Let's stop the quarrelling and use the time better.' He was talking with his lips pressed into her back.

She forced the smile from her lips and turned to him, 'Jo just draw up the zip.'

'All right, tonight we'll start from right here.' He dug his finger gently in her lower back. He felt her shudder and smiled.

'You are still as lovely as the day I set eyes on you, you know?'

She smiled at him from her mirror.

'You and your sweet mouth.'

'You know I mean it, you shape is the same.'

'You don't have to exaggerate.'

'It is!' He cocked his head to one side, licking his lips.

'My waist was twenty-two inches then.'

'Well it is that still.'

She shook her head, 'You must be blind.' She rested her powder puff down and pressed her stomach in.

'Anyway I love it. I can't keep my hand off it.' He made to get up again.

'Joseph, sit down! I have things to do.'

He stood up anyway, rubbed her neck, then walked over to the window that looked out on to their garden. 'About Esmine. I just have to say one more thing to defend myself . . .'

'Oh Joseph, I have to hurry up and you have to get some sleep, you are the one who is on night shift this week. Is it twelve hours or eight this time?'

He ran his hands over his face, 'Twelve, eight to eight. But I'm going to try and get one of me mate Lenny to change with me so I can do days from Monday. You want us to be together you said.'

He had to stop himself reaching out to her again, first to touch her face then to unzip the dress he had just zipped up. 'I have to say

46

just one thing. You are good at making me feel that I am the only one who show preference. Esmine has always been the apple of your eye.' He turned to look at her, his conscience a little eased just by saying that.

'You know that is not true! I only try to make up because of the way you carry on. You have always taken this thing about your *first born* too far . . .'

Joseph shook his head and made to defend himself.

His wife dared him with her widened eyes to speak, so he contented himself with a smile as he sat back on the bed.

'. . . And the worst thing, Joy is just like you. She looks like you, she talks like you. She loves to hear the sound of her own voice like you and she's strong like you. She doesn't need pampering and protecting, but Esmine does. Joy will always be all right'. She sighed. 'I'm not so sure about Esmine.'

'I don't like that look that keeps coming in your eyes you know Beatrice. I keep telling you.' He got up again and stood behind her, resting his hands on her shoulders.

'I don't know why you don't stop your foolishness. I don't know what look you keep talking about.' She noticed that he had his head cocked to one side – that look that said he had better sense than to believe her – but she would not let him see that she had noticed.

He shook his head and sat down again.

She sighed, her voice quiet when she spoke again. 'All I'm asking you is tonight . . . this week . . . at the dining table, sit next to Esmine and remember that you have two children not one. You hear me Jo?'

He grunted and pursed his lips.

'Please sweetheart. I may not always be around to make up to Esmine.'

'Bea, honey, don't make it sound so bad. I love both of my children.'

'I know you do, but you have something more for Joy and if you

47

can admit it you'll at least try to be careful not to push Esmine out.'

Meals were not staggered that week. They ate together and talked late into the nights.

'I'm glad Lenny changed shifts with you Jo,' Beatrice said.

'Well, I've done it for him often enough. He couldn't say no. I'll do his shift after we come back from Birmingham.' He looked across the table at Joy, 'You remember we going up to see Lenford on Saturday?'

Joy nodded and continued eating, still puzzled about why her father had asked her to change her usual seat at the table. She had managed to get there before Esmine, who had raised her eyebrow but said nothing when she had found her seat beside her mother occupied.

'We can't put if off again; Lenford say he has a lot for me to help him with.' Joseph licked his lips. 'The food is good Bea. You really excelling youself this week.'

'You saying that I'm not usually a good cook?' Beatrice smiled across the table at him but rested her eyes on Esmine. She felt good. They had all kept their word to her and the week was going well.

'Of course I'm not saying that, but this week you cook as if we celebrating Christmas.'

'It was a good idea, Mummy, for us to eat together this week. I've got into the habit of eating on the run. It's nice to sit and eat . . .'

Her mother smiled, '. . . and to talk. That was what I wanted more than anything.'

'You look more rested as well Mummy but still . . .'

'I feel all right Esmine dear.' She reached across the table and stroked Esmine's hand, 'Are *you* all right?'

'Mummy, you've asked me that every day this week . . .'

Joy smirked. 'Don't you know, Sis, Mummy always thinks you need looking after?' She looked at her mother. 'You have to stop treating Esmine like a baby you know Mummy, she is twenty-one.'

'Joy, just be quiet! You don't complain when Daddy treats you like a baby.'

'The both of you carry on like babies sometimes,' Beatrice interrupted.

'Don't worry with them, you hear, Bea? One minute they carrying on like puss and dog, the next minute they wrap up and tied up and we can't get a strand of hair between them . . .' Joseph looked around the table at the three of them. 'Anyway, I wanted to have *my* little say tonight.'

Beatrice made a face. 'How you mean tonight? You always have your say. You mean the rest of us have to fight to get a word in.'

He cleared his throat. 'What I was going to say is that now that the girls have finished their studies, we should start thinking seriously about going back home.'

Joy's heart stopped and she couldn't look up from her plate. She had not expected him to raise this now. He hadn't even mentioned it to her for months. She felt herself sinking with her mother's long sigh.

'How you mean you and I should start? You have never stopped and as I often times tell you I am not going to uproot again.' She held his eyes. 'Especially now! This is the time I've been waiting for all these years. When we first came to England . . . In those days we were in Egbaston.' She looked across at her daughters, 'Just near where your Uncle Lenford lives. I hated it when the white people used to make me feel like a stray dog, like we didn't belong here, *cussing us to go back to our own country*!' A deep sadness came into her eyes. 'In those days I saw the time when my children, who I knew would be born here, saying to those very same people, and others like them, *This is where I was born! This is where I belong!*'

There was a silence when she stopped speaking. Finally Joseph spoke, 'I think I understand what you saying but I want you please to hear me out for a minute.' He pressed her hand to his lips. 'White people will never accept us. We could be born and reborn here a million times. So there is no point in staying in this God-forsaken place. They wring us dry already . . . we give everything we have to give. We punish enough dearheart!'

Beatrice sighed and shifted around in her chair. But Joseph persisted undeterred, 'I really think we should try and go home and rest for our last few years.'

Beatrice shook her head slowly.

Esmine leapt in. 'Oh Daddy, I thought you had stopped dreaming.' Her voice was as set as her mother's face.

Joy pounced on her, 'Why do you call it a dream? This place can never be my home . . . My days here are definitely numbered.'

'Don't be so melodramatic Joy. Daddy wasn't talking about *you* going anywhere,' she looked sceptically at her sister. 'This is your home. You *don't* have to agree with everything Daddy wants to do, you know.'

Out of the corner of her eye Joy caught her parents exchanging glances, but her tone was no less cutting than her sister's had been. 'Out of touch as usual. Girl you are in for some very rude awakening when you start living in the real world.'

Joy found herself expecting the warm hand of her father's on hers, then realised she was on the wrong side of the table. She raised and dropped her shoulders.

Beatrice sighed, looking at her husband, 'I just think we have to be realistic. We uproot once already. I can't see what good it will serve us if we uproot again.' Her voice seemed tired all of a sudden.

Joseph thought for a moment and then spoke more softly than before, 'What you must remember though, I didn't want to come to this place, and after quarter of a century I don't think any different.'

Beatrice lapsed into furious silence, her face rigid with annoyance.

Joy intervened, 'Mummy you said this is a week for talking and I have always said I would come to some decision when I had finished my studies. Well, I've finished.'

Esmine's voice was as determined as her sister's. 'Joy that was years ago. Many things have happened since then.'

Joy ignored her. '*I* meant it then, Mummy, and I mean it now.'

'*I* would like you all to listen to *me* now.' They all looked at Joseph, his voice demanding attention.

'What I know is that I would not want to die in this place.' His voice changed and it became like a gentle breeze, blowing for itself, oblivious of the way it swayed the trees and made babies catch their breath. 'Sometimes me whole body go cold at the thought of dying here. I can't stand the thought of being buried in this cold, cold place. No, no I would not want that at all, I want to be buried on the old land by the rest of the old people. But if Satan is bad enough to let me die here, of this one thing I'm sure! As soon as the preacherman says, *dust to dust*, this very carcass of mine,' he prodded his chest, 'will pick up speed and fly back to where my mama buried my navel string. The black man spirit doesn't belong in this place.'

Beatrice looked hard at him. She was emphatic when she spoke and she looked only at him. 'I really don't think that you should put that kind of pressure on the girls. Suppose they can't manage it?' She stopped and waited.

Their eyes held.

He said nothing, just waited for her to continue. 'It cost a lot to ship bodies home you know and what is the point anyway? When you are dead, you're dead. You won't be the wiser, and even if you were, I doubt if you'd care where they putting your body'.

When she stopped speaking and he was sure she was finished, he spoke. 'How you mean pressure on the girls? Where are *you* going to be?'

Joy moved about in her chair. 'I hate this conversation.

51

Everybody is making all these assumptions. *Nobody* is going to die.' She shook her body irritably.

Esmine looked across at her, 'For once I agree with you Joy.'

But their parents did not hear them.

Beatrice spoke as if only to her husband, 'You know the only reason why I would go back Jo is because since the day we set foot in this place, you've been blaming me for coming here.' She shook her head. 'That is the only reason why I would go back.'

She stopped and looked from Joy to Esmine, drawing their attention to her, 'But one thing I'm saying if I drop dead tomorrow. *I do not want anybody to ship this carcass out of here.*'

Esmine made a face, 'Oh Mummy, don't.' She looked to Joy who nodded agreement.

Beatrice smiled, 'Darling. I'm just saying. It's a waste of money and time.' She laughed but it wasn't a convincing laugh. 'Anyway, that will be the one time that they won't say we don't really belong here. When you dead.' She laughed again. 'They either give you the plot of land or they keep you to stink up the place.'

Esmine wasn't amused. 'Oh Mummy, please.'

'All right Esmine.'

Joseph sighed long and hard. 'Well I am learning something today. You really trap me now.' He looked briefly at Joy but rested his eyes on his wife. 'You know that the last thing I would want is to go home and leave you here whether I'm dead or living.'

Joy and Esmine exchanged glances. Joy shook her head. It was not like him to sound so defeated, to capitulate, not on that, not on the hope that was dearer to him than life. What was going on? No one knew more than she that her father lived for the day when her mother would at least concede the possibility that she would go back to Jamaica.

So, it was all a game to him. He didn't mean any of it! My God, he didn't mean any of it! All of it just talk.

Joy got up to clear the table. She put the plates on the draining board and leaned with her back against the sink. Her mother was *still* not on their side, and she did not seem persuadable. But worse than that, her father had just thrown it all in without really trying.

If there had been a way out of the kitchen without going back through the dining room Joy would have taken it. She didn't want to go back there just yet. She had never felt so alone in her life. For the first time she realised that her father was not on her side, and it confused her because she didn't understand how he had come to change so much.

Her father called to her, 'Honeybunch, what are you doing in the kitchen so long?' His voice was strained.

'I'm coming.' She picked the dishes up again and made a noise as if she was arranging them, wondering all the time whether he remembered their conversation five years ago as clearly as she did. It could have been yesterday.

She braced herself and went back into the dining room to take her place by her mother.

Beatrice touched Joy's hand gently but was looking at her husband. 'I'm glad that we settled everything this week.'

Joseph sighed and changed position in his chair. 'Like what dearheart?'

Joy continued to look down at the table.

'Well, we decided that we are all here to stay. I'm glad we are not in limbo anymore.' And then in a quieter voice, 'Jamaica has been like a weight around our necks for too long.'

Joy raised her eyes slowly from the table to see her father look away from her. 'Mummy, I don't think *we* decided anything. *You* did.'

'Joy don't be rude!' Esmine glared at her.

'Shut up Esmine.'

'The both of you rest for a minute,' Beatrice ordered. 'We said we'd come to some decision when both of you finish your studies . . .'

Joy looked across at her.

She was serious, 'Well now you've finished.' She smiled at Esmine. You've both got you jobs . . . And now I don't see any sense in keeping false hope alive.' She sighed.

'I see,' Joseph cleared his throat and rubbed his nose. 'So you believe we have settled it then?'

Beatrice was emphatic, 'Of course! When we came back from holiday just before Joy went off to university we fell out about it. One of us has to make a decision. I don't *ever* want this family to split up . . .' She looked around at all of them, her eyes resting on Esmine, who was smiling triumphantly.

'Joseph I hope you agree with what I said?', she turned challenging eyes to her husband.

'I agree that a family is not a family if they all over the place. We already gone through that.' He shook his head, 'My parents died alone when I was here slaving for the white man. And me one brother Lenford planning to go to America. What kind of life is it when families don't want to stick together? We have to all stick together now. But . . .'

'Joseph! No buts please. We are deciding *now*!' Beatrice held his eyes. 'Unless of course you want to leave me here?'

It was more a statement of conclusion than a question, and the weight of it silenced him.

Joy felt for him then.

'Sweetheart? You know it hurts me when you talk like that.' He tried to smile at her but only a faint tremor passed over his lips.

As if to heal the wound she reached across the table and stroked his hand. 'I know it's hard Jo. I know the hope is what's kept you going all these years . . .'

'Yes.' His voice and eyes were distant and for one moment Joy saw the same glazed expression on his face that had been in her mother's eyes all week. It made Joy shudder with confusion. She looked to Esmine but she was not on her side; she was not even looking at Joy.

'Yes!' he repeated. 'I can't lie about that.' He sighed deeply, 'When we came I was shocked by all the ill treatment.' He spoke very quietly, 'But we had paid our passage, given away everything we had, so we *had* to put up with it, the abuse and the insults . . .'

Joy looked across and met his eyes.

Her father's voice was charged with such pain and she was helpless to alleviate it.

Only her mother had such power.

Joy looked across at her, struggling to dispell the rising anger and bitterness she felt towards her. *She has taken this thing too far.*

Her mother showed no sign of uncertainty. Her posture was, as it always was, straight but relaxed.

Joy shook her head, giving way to the overwhelming anger she felt. She forgot about her concern for her mother's well-being, her concern about the look they had all noticed in her eyes.

It's not Daddy's fault. As usual he's just trying to keep peace. She's tricked him. Yes, that's what she's done! She's pretended to be ill or tired or whatever and tricked him into capitulating! She's used his devotion to her, his reluctance to argue, to fight . . .

What Joy saw now was her father's look of total defeat and loss. A look that Joy had thought never to see on his face. She tried to reach him with her eyes but he was far away.

Now that he had capitulated on the one thing that had kept him going for the twenty-six years he had been in England, Joy wondered if anything could ever make him smile again.

Four

The following day their mother spent the day cleaning the house and would not accept that it was unusual to do it on a Thursday. 'Well, since I'm off work I thought I'd get things together.'

Joseph had not come home yet and she had asked Joy and Esmine to sit with her in their bedroom. She had a trunk opened and was kneeling by it.

'Why are you opening the trunk Mummy?' Esmine stretched out on the floor.

Joy adopted the lotus position next to her, watching her mother taking papers out, untying bundles and rearranging them.

'I just need to sort these out and show both of you where everything is.' She looked at Esmine, 'I know *you* know what's in it but I don't think Joy does.'

Joy raised an eyebrow and shook her head.

'You know your daddy believes in keeping everything.' She picked up a large envelope. 'This one has all your school reports right from infant school.' She handed it to Esmine who smiled in recognition.

She sifted through and gave another to Joy. It was a bundle of her reports from secondary school.

She handed a large envelope to Esmine, 'And this one has both your O and A level certificates.'

Joy looked at them without interest.

Esmine sat up, 'Wow! We haven't seen these for ages . . .'

'I have never looked at them.' The resentment in Joy's voice was obvious.

Her mother took her hand out of the trunk for a moment, 'Oh! You were always out when Esmine and I went through the trunk, dear.'

'Or you were never interested,' Esmine snapped.

Joy shrugged.

Her mother took out a small bundle of old school magazines. She handed them to Joy, 'And these are the school magazines with essays and poetry that you wrote. One of them has the speech you gave when you stood for head girl. And one has you acceptance speech.' She stroked Joy's face with the back of her hand.

Joy looked down at her folded knees and sighed.

Beatrice put all the bundles back in the trunk. 'Everything is in here.' Esmine stretched out on the floor again. Joy kept her lotus position.

'One day I want the both of you to go through them together. All our insurance papers are in here too. The deed for the house back home and title for the properties in St John's Road and St Mary.'

'We'll never need them,' Esmine said as she pulled up her legs and extended them again.

'You may not, but just in case.' Her mother sighed put down the paper she was looking at and looked from Esmine to Joy.

She bent and kissed Joy on the forehead, looked at her, then hugged her, 'I do love you Joy. Don't ever forget that. One day I hope you'll understand me.'

Her mother's smile was gentle and a wave of guilt swept over Joy for the anger she had been harbouring since the night before. But she still couldn't respond.

Beatrice closed the trunk, stood up and rubbed her knees, then sat on the bed. 'How *is* Lee, Joy?'

'Oh, he's all right.'

'Still desperate for you eh?'

'Of course he is Mummy, but you know Joy. One minute she's hot the next minute she's cold. She doesn't know what she wants . . .'

Joy looked at her sister and tutted.

Esmine was partly right. When she had met Lee at university she had meant the relationship to be for that time and place. Since then she had managed to ward off his constant plans for their marriage but was no more free from pressure, and guilt.

Beatrice bent and rubbed Joy's forehead, 'Don't mind Esmine, you hear? Just go along with what you think is right my dear.'

She ran her hand across Joy's and Esmine's shoulders and sighed, 'Whatever happens though, you two must try to live good. That is what's important. I don't worry about either of you and men . . . You both see how me and your daddy live.' She ran her fingers across her lips. 'Whatever differences we have you can still see that we love and respect each other.' She stopped and looked at both of them. Joy holding her lotus position, her head down. Esmine, her eyes fixed on her mother.

She looked from Esmine to Joy. 'I'll always be happy if you will decide for yourselves what is best for you and stick to it.'

When she spoke again her eyes were still. 'Don't ever let a man think that you are desperate for him, that your life depends on him. Both of you have your education. This is not the olden times days when women needed men to provide for them.' She smiled then and moved her eyes from Esmine to Joy.

Joy's heart melted some more with the guilt that she had felt before. Their mother's voice was firm when she spoke again, 'Whatever else you may need a man for, it is not to give you status, food and clothes. You can both give yourselves that and more.' She sighed, stood up, rubbed her knees and walked to the door. 'Let's go and cook some food you hear? I want to make something nice for your father tonight.'

Joy lifted herself from the lotus position, helped her sister up, and together they followed their mother through the dining room into the kitchen.

That night there was still a strain and it seemed to Joy that everyone was careful not to raise the question of Jamaica. She was glad because she hoped to get some time with her father alone before it came up again.

She planned it for Sunday. Her parents would be going to see her Uncle Lenford on Saturday, so it would have to be Sunday. She would have to make up some excuse to go for a drive with him. She could tell he too needed to talk.

On the Friday night, while they sat half-watching television, their father reminded them not to expect them back from Birmingham until late on Saturday.

'Now I wish we didn't have to go tomorrow'. He looked at his wife. 'But Lenford and I have few things we have to discuss.'

Beatrice sighed, 'Lenford always wants us to do the travelling and I really don't feel like travelling meself.'

'You can stay you know. I can just run up there by myself.'

'No. It wouldn't look good. I'll go. I promised to do some shopping with Sarah so I can't let her down.' She shook her head. 'I just have a funny feeling.'

'I'll go if you don't feel like going,' Joy offered, anxious now to be supportive of her mother. 'You can have a rest. I'll go with Daddy.' It only occurred to Joy then that it would be the ideal opportunity to speak to him. 'Yes Mother, you stay. I'd love to go.'

'No dear. You need the rest more than me.'

Joseph stood up. 'Let's get an early night anyway.' He reached out and helped his wife up. Beatrice turned and looked at her daughters. 'Goodnight girls. I love you both.' She squeezed her husband's hands, released them and walked back to her daughters. 'You two try and show one another your love, you hear? We are a small family and we need to be together.' She hugged Esmine and then Joy.

'Come on dearheart, the girls are all right,' but he moved over to them, 'I suppose since we all making confessions tonight let me tell you two that I love the both of you too.' He touched Esmine's chin before kissing her on the forehead.

He turned to Joy. If they had been in St John's Road, and back in the days before they ran electricity through the town, the peenie-whallies would have flashed round them, making the pitch blackness light up like day. But they were not in St John's Road, there were no fireflies about. They were only in their front room in London town with her mother and sister standing round them. But Joy found herself squinting anyway, such was the brightness of the gaze that he gave her. He hugged her.

As Beatrice and Esmine turned to walk though the door, he said, 'Keep heart Joy. It only takes one of us . . .'

'Jo, come on please.' Beatrice's voice was sharp.

'Coming dearheart.' He turned back to Joy. 'You hear me sweetheart.'

Joy could hear her mother and Esmine going up the steps. 'Daddy, I hear you but we must talk . . . I don't know what's going on . . . One minute . . .'

'On Sunday, we'll go for a drive out . . .'

'That's what I thought we could do.'

'Joseph!'

They both turned to the door.

'Coming up now dearheart.' He turned back to Joy again.

'Okay Daddy, goodnight.'

He squeezed her hand and turned, 'Goodnight Joy.'

Joy stood where he left her and listened to his footsteps go up the steps. Sighing, she went down to the kitchen to make herself camomile tea.

When she got up in the night she heard her father's voice and her mother's laughter drifting through the door.

It reminded her of the days when, as a child, she had tried to sneak into their room and found it locked. As in those days, their voices conjured up an image of them flying together on clouds. Despite the night chill of late September and the weight of uncertainty she felt, their voices warmed her as she crept back into her room.

Five

Joy looked at the clock on the mantelpiece when the door bell rang at 9 p.m. She had been reading the newspaper. Frowning, she went to answer it. Esmine had just gone up to have a bath.

Neither of them was expecting anyone. Joy opened the door and faced two police officers.

'Oh! What can I do for you?'

'Who is it Joy?' Esmine called.

'One *minute* Esmine!'

'Are you Miss Brown?' the WPC asked.

'Yes.'

'Who is that Sis? Is it Lee?'

'Esmine, I said hold *on*!'

'I'm Sergeant Ward and this is WPC Reeves. Can we come in please?'

'Why?' Joy looked from one to the other.

Sergeant Ward rested his hand on the door and gently pushed it back.

'What the hell are you doing?' Joy shouted.

'Joy, what is it?'

Joy turned, looked briefly up the steps, then turned back to the officers without replying.

The police officers looked at each other. WPC Reeves spoke, 'Miss Brown we need to have a word.'

'Why?' She held her eyes.

'Joy who is that? Didn't you hear me call out to you?'

Joy turned to watch Esmine come down the steps in her dressing gown.

She made to tell her to go back and put some clothes on but was interrupted by Sergeant Ward, 'I'm afraid we *do* need to come in young ladies.'

'Joy! Police! What do they want?'

Esmine's voice was confusing Joy.

The officers stepped into the hall, simultaneously taking off their caps and holding them to their chests.

'What are you doing in our house? I don't remember saying . . .'

The officers stepped past her. 'Is that the sitting room?' Sergeant Ward pointed to the door nearest them, 'Please go in there, we need to talk to you.'

Joy and Esmine looked at each other then led them in.

'I think you should sit down please,' WPC Reeves encouraged.

'Don't order us around in . . .' Joy began.

Esmine touched her sister's arm. Joy looked at her and they both abruptly sat down.

The officers took the sofa on the other side of the room. 'Have you got a neighbour or anyone who can be with you?' Sergeant Reeves looked from Joy to Esmine.

'What?' Joy looked puzzled. 'Whatever would we need a neighbour for? Perhaps you can just tell us what this is all about. We are busy, our parents are expected back any minute now and I would certainly not like them to find you here . . .'

WPC Reeves reddened and looked down at her hands.

Joy looked back at Esmine, then turned to face them again, irritated and annoyed '*What is it?*'

'Oh God, Joy, something is wrong.' Esmine sprang up.

'Sit down . . . Please!'

Esmine sat down, her eyes wide.

Joy did not budge. 'What the hell is it?'

'I am sorry.' Sergeant Ward looked from Joy to Esmine.

Esmine stiffened.

'I am very sorry,' he began again. 'We have to tell you that your parents were involved in an accident, a car accident.'

Joy felt for a moment that the world had stopped and then begun suddenly to spin. Her whole body was spinning with it.

'My God! Mummy,' Joy heard herself shout as her mother's vacant eyes flashed in front of her.

Esmine jumped up, '*No! No! No! Mummy.*'

WPC Reeves got up, lowered her back on to the settee and sat next to her.

'My God.' Joy stared into the sergeant's face. 'Was it serious?'

The officer facing her cleared his throat and clutched his cap closer to his chest.

'Please? Are they all right?'

'Oh Joy,' Esmine's voice was hoarse.

Joy turned briefly to look at her, then back to the officer. 'Was it serious? They are all right aren't they?'

'I'm afraid it was a serious accident. It was fatal.'

Esmine jumped up again, 'Oh, oh God, no . . .'

Joy leapt to her.

'Another car crossed the central reservation.'

Joy heard his voice as if it were far away. She saw the policeman's red face, heard faint mumbled sounds from his radio, but they were drowned out by the picture of her mother's face and eyes. Mummy had known she was going to die. She had known! Oh God, that was what it was all about.

'Which hospital is Daddy in?'

Esmine was sobbing, 'Mummy, No!'

WPC Reeves cleared her throat, 'The accident was very serious.'

'Oh please tell me which hospital he's in . . .' Joy's knees were weak.

'I'm sorry, but . . . but they were *both* killed.'

When he stopped, everything else stopped too. Joy's heart, her mind, her ability to think.

Then came the loudest, most piercing howl she had ever heard. It was like something coming from inside her. She touched her face but it was dry. Then she realised that it was Esmine.

She had not felt Esmine pull away from her but now she was standing in the middle of the room with her hands pressing into her eyes and screaming at the very top of her voice. Her voice came out first as a desperate piercing scream then a fading whimper.

'No, no, they can't be dead! You liar! Liar! Oh God! Mummy. Mummy! Daddy . . .y . . .y'

Joy, paralysed, watched, but could not help her. The WPC held her for a while, then gently pushed her to her seat, and seemed in no time to have produced blankets and hot, sweet tea.

Sergeant Ward addressed Joy, 'You'll need to identify the bodies . . .'

Joy bit her lips and looked around the room.

'There's no hurry love. When you're ready . . .'

Joy nodded.

The WPC chipped in. 'Let me get a neighbour for you. Who are you close to on the road? Shall I try next door?'

Joy frowned, 'No, no. I'll call my boyfriend . . . Lee. He'll come. I'll call him. Thank you. Which hospital . . .?'

Sergeant Ward wrote down the details. She thanked them again as he handed her the note.

'Shall we wait?' The sergeant was looking more uncomfortable by the second.

Joy just wanted them out. 'No. No. Please, we'll be all right.'

She didn't wait to see them out. 'Come and lie on the bed upstairs Essy.'

'We'll show ourselves out love.' The sergeant led the way to the door.

Joy pulled her sister up from the floor and supported her up the stairs.

'Joy it can't be true. It can't.'

'Sheee . . .'

'It can't be . . .'

As they passed their parents' room Esmine's weight seemed to increase on her. Joy sighed as she looked at their closed door. There were no voices, no giggles, just stillness.

Joy helped her sister into the bed and stood over her, listening to her sobbing. Then she sat, slowly, and waited for Esmine to calm. Her legs began to numb and gradually that numbness spread, until she was oblivious to even Esmine's continuing wails.

Eventually she pulled herself up. Everything was as it had been. Her sister was still whimpering and deep, deep inside her, there was still that voice saying. *It can't be. Not my father.*

'Esmine. I will have to go and make some calls.'

Esmine looked at her vacantly.

It was after eleven. Joy called the hospital first. She did it all with an odd, quiet calm, as if she was someone else making arrangements to view strange bodies in an unknown morgue.

She called her uncle Lenford and listened to him screaming down the phone, not able to make him feel better, to convince him then that it was not his fault.

'Yes we are going to identify the bodies now . . . We'll be fine until you come . . . Why don't you leave it until tomorrow? Okay. If you think you are all right to drive. I'm going to call Lee, he'll come with us . . . Yes I think they've got the right people . . .'

Lee arrived sooner than she had expected. When she opened the door to him, she suddenly noticed his resemblance to her father.

He held her, without speaking.

Six

Joy awoke to a heavy stillness in the house. She listened for the familiar sounds of morning, her father's laugh, her mother running her bath, snatches of conversation.

Then she remembered. The weight of grief settled on her again. She wanted to hug herself, to scream and howl. But she had to be strong. She had to hold together. She had to be in control. There was Esmine to think of, plans for the funeral.

She heard sounds from downstairs. For a moment her heart leapt, then she remembered. Her uncle and his wife had arrived some while after they had returned from the hospital.

She felt the bed move and braced herself. She turned to face her sister. She reached out to her, and, immediately, Esmine began to cry.

'Esmine sweetheart. You are going to make yourself ill if you carry on like that.' She cradled her sister, listening to her sobbing, realising fully that she would now have to be mother and father as well as sister to her.

A steady stream of visitors came to the house as the day went on. Joy had to speak to them while Esmine sat in the corner of the sitting room in tears. News of their parents' deaths spread fast and soon the house was full of shocked friends, the smells of the food they had brought with them: the curried goat and fried chicken, and the rum.

Joy mingled with them, talking, explaining, sympathising with their tears, their weeping, their disbelief. But every sound resonated in her head, irritating her and making her long for them to go. If only they knew what she was thinking. All they could see was how strong she was. 'Just like her father,' they whispered to each other.

Towards evening her Aunt Sarah and Uncle Lenford took the girls aside to discuss the funeral. The only free room was their parents' bedroom.

Joy didn't want to go in there, but she gritted her teeth and entered, sitting with Esmine at the foot of the bed, leaning against the trunk.

Aunt Sarah sat on the bed by her husband. Joy wanted to snarl at them, to tell them that her mother didn't like other people sitting on her bed. But she bit back her words.

Aunt Sarah spoke, 'Girls, had your parents expressed any wish about where they wanted to be . . . to be laid to rest?' She looked to her husband but he was looking firmly at the carpet.

Joy sighed, 'Daddy would have liked more than anything in the world to go back . . .'

'Joy please! Don't!' Esmine's voice rose sharply and as Joy looked at her she knew Esmine would keep her father to the promise he had made to her mother.

So Joy couldn't contradict her. She watched her sister's grief-stricken face and knew she couldn't even remind her of how the light had gone out of their father's face when he had made that promise. So Joy bit her lips and the well within her deepened.

'Esmine dear, what were you going to say?'

Esmine looked away from her aunt to her sister. 'Mummy and Daddy said that they would always stay together.'

'What do you mean dear?' Aunt Sarah lowered her voice.

Esmine continued looking straight into her sister's eyes, 'Mummy knew . . . I'm sure she did . . . and the night before . . . she got Daddy to say . . . to promise us that we were all here to stay . . . that the family would all stay together. They have to be buried here. I need to be near . . .'

Joy could no longer meet her sister's eyes. She watched her dissolving in tears. But she couldn't reach out to her then.

'Joy?' Uncle Lenford spoke for the first time. 'You Mummy and Daddy spoke about it? And she *persuaded* him?' His surprise showed through his confusion.

Aunt Sarah knelt and wrapped Esmine in her arms, resting her head against her chest.

Joy looked at her uncle, then back at Esmine, reading the challenge in her sister's eyes. And Joy found herself nodding to her uncle's question and seeing as she did so, a sudden image of her father's face dropping.

'I see . . . I see . . .' Uncle Lenford shook his head.

Joy had to get out of the room. She stood up, her legs shaking. She walked heavily out of the room, carrying the weight of her betrayal.

Seven

Janet had the same dream every night. She was back on the tube, going to work. From the moment she entered the carriage, she felt conspicuous. So she sat, with her legs crossed tightly, her arms folded, looking at nobody. Avoiding their eyes. But eventually she dared to glance upward. She caught a man staring at her. She looked away quickly, thinking he'd do the same. But she felt his eyes, intense and piercing. She got up, hoping to move to the other side of the carriage, to get away from the heat of his gaze. It was then that she realised who he was. *That* man. That man again. And, like the other times, he wasn't the only one looking at her. They were *all* staring at her! She scurried along the aisle expecting to get out at the next station, only to see it flash past. She rushed instead towards the door at the end of the carriage but the other passengers stood up in unison behind her. Running through the carriages, fumbling with the interconnecting doors, she could *feel* them gaining on her. She could see the end of the train. There was the figure of a man waiting for her. A guard? She ran towards him, overcome with relief. But as she came closer she saw his face. Her father! Unable to stop running, she was propelled towards him, as he raised his arms threateningly above his head. With a start, she awoke . . .

The fight with her father had been the beginning of her end. She

70

went to the doctor and explained to him that she was having terrible dreams. He gave her pills. She didn't take them. The dreams got worse. As soon as she fell asleep they would come. She would try switching the lights on, the radio, reading passages from the Bible. But to no avail. Eventually in desperation she tried to stay awake. But she would invariably fall asleep again and there she would be on the tube. She stopped getting into bed at nights. She sat on the sofa, the Bible by one side, a hymn book on the other, gospel music blaring out. When she was unbearably tired, she paced the room screaming the twenty-third psalm at the top of her voice. Or singing, joining the voices on the tape. But sooner or later she fell exhausted on to the sofa and slept and dreamt.

She went back to the doctor, insisting that he do something about the dreams. He didn't seem more interested than he had been the first time, especially when she told him she had not taken the drugs. 'I don't like the idea of mood-changing drugs,' she ventured.

He looked down at the prescription he had just taken out, 'I really don't know what you expect me to do if you're not prepared to co-operate.'

Janet pressed her hands in her lap, close to tears.

The doctor softened his tone, 'I'll refer you to the outpatient department at the psychiatric hospital . . . They will take it from there.'

Janet stared at him – a *psychiatric hospital! I'm not mad!*

'You'll get a letter from them with an appointment.'

She got up and left the surgery with no intention of keeping any appointment, and feeling more desperate than before.

She put off calling Esmine for as long as she could. She didn't want to burden her so soon after her parents' death. But each day she felt more panicked than before. She didn't have the energy to do anything. She phoned in sick at work and sat in her flat, sandwiched between her hymn book and her Bible, eating only when hunger pains became unbearable.

It was Esmine who eventually called, not having heard from her in weeks. She immediately recognised something was wrong and said she would call to see her.

Later that day, Janet watched from behind her bedroom curtains as Esmine's car pulled up outside the large Victorian house.

Esmine was amazed by Janet's appearance. Her clothes were crumpled and dirty, her hair unkempt, her eyes bloodshot and puffy, large dark circles underneath. 'God, Janet, what's the matter?'

Janet shook her head and burst into tears.

Esmine held her as they went up the stairs. The room was a mess too, plates with scraps of food, half-empty cups, dirty clothes, were strewn across the floor. The bed was unmade, the duvet and sheets trailing down the side. She knew that Janet had been depressed for some time but had hardly had time to sort out her own problems, let alone find time to support her. Esmine suddenly felt guilty for not having made time for her friend.

She lowered Janet gently on the sofa and sat with her as she sobbed, unable to make sense of what she was saying. Eventually she made tea and suggested afterwards that they went out for a walk in the park. She helped Janet to wash and change, and gently plaited her hair for her.

They walked towards the local park, silent for most of the way.

'I can't go on like this Esmine, I can't.'

Esmine strung their arms together, not knowing what to say to her.

'The doctor thinks I'm going off my head you know. Do *you* think I'm going mad Esmine?'

'No. Of course not,' was all she could manage.

Janet continued as if she had not heard her 'They brought me up to believe that God is good,' her shoulders dropped forward, 'but now all I can see is evil. Why is there so much evil around me?'

Esmine fingered her earrings and tried to assure her that there was nothing evil about her, that she was just upset because her parents were not speaking to her. She tried to persuade her that as soon as she was able to sleep normally she would start to see everything differently.

'I will never be able to get a good night's sleep. How can I with those dreams? With those people watching me?' She paused, then said very quietly, 'It's as if Daddy has prayed for them to spy on me.'

Esmine shook her head and squeezed their arms together.

Janet stopped. 'He did say that when you dishonour your parents all kind of pestilence come upon you. A millstone is hung around your neck.'

'Janet you must never believe that. It's nonsense.'

'It's not. That's what's happening to me. I dishonoured them.' They started to walk again.

'Janet! Listen to me!' Esmine stopped, resting her arms around Janet's shoulders and turning her round to face her, 'You must stop making yourself believe all that. You have done nothing to bring this upon yourself. Nothing. *Do you hear me*?'

Janet looked at her, but it may have been at something else, very far away.

'You don't understand either . . .'

Esmine let her arms drop but kissed her on the forehead.

They sat by the duck pond, a line of anglers nearby, in fixed concentration. Esmine fingered her earrings, the light wind playing with her hair. She smoothed her hair from her face, throwing her head back impatiently. She wanted so much to do something to help her friend. Especially now that she understood what endless pain and unhappiness meant.

Janet looked into the water. She tensed and shivered, looking away, not able to block out her father's voice. His prophecy of her drowning. She wiped away the beads of perspiration forming on her forehead. The water was almost still. 'And to think I used to love water.'

'Umm. Why *used* to?'

'It reminded me of my mum and having a bath when I was young. But . . .' she stopped.

'But what?' Esmine pressed.

Janet sighed and shook her head.

Esmine didn't think she should force her to talk. They were quiet for a long time.

'Janet?' Esmine faced her, the earlier irritation gone from her voice, 'Do you think now that you should go back. I mean try and see if it may help?'

Janet bit on the inside of her cheek and Esmine caught a sudden glimpse of a dimple. It seemed incongruous in a face that had forgotten how to smile.

'That won't help. To Daddy repentance comes before for-giveness . . . and I have sinned . . . Unpardonable sins . . . Commiting myself, dishonouring them.' Janet raised her shoulders in a sigh.

'But you said you weren't doing anything with Roger.'

'I wasn't.' Janet spoke quietly, 'That's not the point. *He* thought I was.'

'Janet! You must separate what is true from what your dad thinks.'

Janet shook her head, 'You don't understand.' She stared at the patterns made by the ducks gliding across the pond. She seemed a long way away.

Esmine turned and rested her hand on Janet's knee. 'You're right. I can't say I understand their behaviour . . .'

Janet looked at her but didn't respond.

Esmine changed the subject, 'Why does the water remind you of your mother?'

Again a faint hint of a smile. 'Would you believe that she used to

74

give me a bath once a week until I was twelve?'

Esmine raised her eyebrow, 'Really?'

Janet nodded, 'Yes. Every Saturday night. She would run the bath for me with bath salt and bubbles. She'd scrub me as we talked,' Janet smiled then.

'That was the only time I could be really by myself with her. The rest of the week she was the pastor's wife.'

A deep sadness came into her eyes. 'No one was allowed to disturb us. Not Daddy. Not my brothers Simon or Luke.' She stopped and sighed. 'They thought that meant that I was her favourite.

'She used to tell me that I could tell her anything then. It was the only place that I knew I *could* tell her everything, ask her anything and it would not get back to Daddy . . . form part of his Sunday sermon.'

'God!' The word slipped out. Esmine grinned apologetically at her friend. Janet looked down at her hands before looking into the pond again. 'It was then that she told me about my periods. I was eleven. She really timed it well because a few weeks later it came. I knew about it before of course but I pretended that I didn't.'

'It was so funny, Esmine, not at the time but looking back. I remembered her saying, "*when it starts you'll be a woman and be able to bear children.*" ' Esmine couldn't help smiling.

'I used to read that word, *bear*, all the time in the Bible but for some reason never guessed what it meant. It was only then that I worked it out. She told me, "*There are men and there are vultures. The vultures are those ones who pounce on any flesh and devour it. The more rotten the flesh the better. They leave their seed wherever they can plant them. They are disgusting filthy dogs.*" '

'You thought they were vultures?' Esmine laughed out.

Janet shook her head. 'Poor animals, eh? Anyway, she said, "*Don't let them get near you. Everything you need is in the Church. Vultures don't survive where there is no rotten flesh. Save yourself. It will be sweeter the longer you wait.*" '

'I hadn't been embarrassed when she had started but as she went on I wanted to sink into the water. Imagine Esmine, the longer you wait the sweeter.'

Esmine laughed out aloud. An angler glanced sharply at her.

'It all seems such a long time ago.' Janet looked down in her lap.

Esmine touched her again, 'My father used to say where there is life there is hope.'

'I wish I could believe that. It seems to be now that life only brings more and more torments.' Janet looked up, focusing on nothing in particular.

Esmine stood up, 'You're tired Jan. Do you want to go now?'

Janet got up, 'Okay.'

They stood facing each other for a moment before Esmine turned. They may have been hewn out of different stones. Esmine walked as if carrying a pitcher of water on her head, her hands swinging by her side. Janet stooped beside her, arms wrapped around her body.

'Jan?'

'Um?' Janet's face had tightened again at the prospect of going back to the flat. She didn't know if she would survive the night alone.

'I've just decided, I'm going to stay with you until you're better.' A great relief surged through Janet. She spun round and hugged Esmine, 'Are you sure?'

'Of course. I can't leave you on your own.'

Janet pulled apart from her, relief replaced by concern. 'But what about Joy? With your parents . . . You know.'

Esmine twisted her earring around in her ear, her smooth unlined forehead creasing in a frown. 'I can't get through to Joy at the moment.' She started to walk again. 'She's so closed in. She doesn't even want to talk about them. About Mummy and Daddy.'

'She's not accepted it, has she?'

Esmine sighed and shook her head, 'I don't know. It's just so hard for me because I want us to be able to talk . . . to cry.' Her eyes clouded over. 'Now I just cry alone in my room and even then I'm frightened that she'll come in and find me . . .'

Janet linked arms with her, 'Give her time,' she suggested, guiltily, realising that she was adding further burden to her friend's heavy load. 'As long as you're sure . . .'

'I am. It will give Joy space. Perhaps that's what she needs.' She turned to look at Janet. 'And besides, you need me . . .'

'Oh Esmine, thank you. I hope one day I'll be able to do for you.'

Esmine squeezed her arm. 'You do for me *now*, believe me Jan.'

As they walked back to the flat, Janet felt the slightest hint of light creeping into her cluttered spirit. But she knew it wouldn't last.

Eight

It was early evening. Joy returned home from work remembering that she had still not posted the letter to her uncle and aunt. She had been carrying it around in her bag for a week. Time was passing so quickly, she could hardly believe it was a year since her parents had died. She was tired but reluctantly walked back to the post box.

Half-way there she noticed two white men coming towards her. Something in their walk made her feel uneasy. Between them they took up the whole pavement and they were talking in whispers as they approached her. Joy ignored her discomfort and continued walking towards them. As she got closer she realised they were not going to move out of the way to let her pass. It crossed her mind to barge through them, but she thought better of it. She was in no mood for a row. She was tired and hungry so she decided to cross. As she did so, one of them said something and they laughed. She kept walking. She didn't even want to meet their eyes, let alone have them brush past her.

She was nearly on the other side when one of them said with purposeful clarity, 'Do you see what I see? A black whore? You don't think she's crossing because of us, do you mate?'

Joy's body tensed. Her fingers tightened into a fist, a wave of anger sweeping through her. How can I walk by and let them get away with that? Let them humiliate me? It flashed across her mind to retrace her steps and face them. She was only half-way across the road, she could still do it.

But she knew better and she continued to walk on, although her head was willing her to look back.

It was then that she felt them coming up behind her. She tried to walk faster, hoping all the time that they were just going about their own business, leaving her to hers. But her legs had suddenly become heavy and she could hardly lift them.

There was no mistaking it. They had turned and were following her. They were just behind her, the quickened thuds of their heavy boots shaking the pavement. Suddenly they were in front of her, legs astride, breathing heavily in her face.

'Where do you think you're going black bitch?'

Joy gulped, her legs shaking. She looked around frantically, hoping to see somebody. Anybody.

The road was still, there was no one in sight. Oh God.

'Me and me friend would like to know why you just crossed the street. He tells me you think we stink.'

Joy's face contorted in anger. She tried to side-step them. Anything but get into an argument.

They moved simultaneously, blocking her, 'You ain't answered us. You ain't going till we get an answer.'

Joy turned to go in the other direction. They jumped in front of her. She looked around desperately.

'It's just you and us blackie. There's nobody around. Nowhere to run to.'

Joy spun round and faced them.

They moved in on her.

She found her voice, 'Get out of my way you dirty . . .'

'Who do you think you're talking to? You ain't going no place, black girl . . . I told you.' His spittle sprayed her face.

Joy stepped back, her heart racing. 'I said get out of my way!'

'We got a right one here. She don't understand English does she?

He's just told you ain't he? We ain't finished with you. We ain't *said* you could go.'

Joy wheeled round to run but one of them grabbed her by the hair and spun her back to face him, 'Where do you think you're going wog?'

She felt her hair coming away from the scalp. She screwed up her face and winced, tears seeping from her eyes. Suddenly, he dragged her face closer to him and brought his head down hard on hers.

The clash of their heads opened Joy's skin. She screamed as his knees came up into the soft of her stomach. Doubled over she didn't see his fist coming for her head again. It knocked her off balance and she fell.

'That's where you belong you dirty wog.' He stood over her, his legs spread.

His friend moved in.

Joy scrambled, trying to get up but a boot kicked her down again. She folded her arms and head inwards, curled in on herself, pain rocking her body. Both of them came at her again, battering her with the furious blows of their boots and fists.

Joy tried to scream but her voice was cracked and weak. She moved her arms frantically, trying hopelessly to block the deluge of blows.

'Oh God help me! Help me!'

'Shut up, you bitch!'

'Shut it!'

'Shut up! Shut up!'

At last she was reduced to a whimpering ball.

'We shut her up.'

'Yeah! We shut up her up . . .'

Joy heard them as if from some distance. There was a strange buzzing in her ears and her body seemed to flutter. Finally, Joy felt a cold wet splatter against her ears and a dampness moving down the side of her neck.

A deep guttural sound and then another splatter on her face, hawk, spit, hawk, spit. Slimey stale lumpy spit sliding over her.

She retched as one of the lumps landed on her mouth. She vomited.

'You disgusting sod . . . She only gone and puked on me boots. You sod.' He kicked her again, his boot connecting with her chin. 'Come on mate! I think we've taught the bitch a lesson.'

'Yeah. We taught her a lesson.'

Joy tried to curl up tighter on the pavement. The buzzing in her ears was louder and she was spinning.

She thought she heard voices. She tensed her body for the kicks. Nothing. Then screams and shouts for help. She tried to blot them out, imagining them to be echoes of her own petrified screams. It was with pained relief that she realised she was drifting into total blackness.

Nine

The death of her parents and the assault were the end of a year that had conspired to make life in England more and more impossible for Joy.

For weeks after she came out of hospital she was petrified of everything that moved. Yet she managed to persuade Esmine to go back to Janet's after only a few days. She needed to be by herself. To go over again and again in her mind the reasons why her life had been so cruel. The only part of it that seemed to be going all right was her work. She had a secure position with a reputable firm of solicitors, but even there, when she looked into the future, she could see little chance for promotion.

Her relationship with her sister had become formal, strained. They seemed able only to go though the motions of the former closeness that had characterised their relationship. They had moved house, unable to bear their old home which reminded them so strongly of their parents. They still lived together and saw each other often, but hardly ever really talked. Each seemed intent on sparing the other. There were so many topics they both had to avoid. So Joy found to her surprise that it was to Lee she turned most often. And even though she knew he bitterly resented being summoned, as he was more often than not, just to relieve her physical tension, he never said no to her.

Joy could only occasionally muster the energy to really be with him. Usually she didn't want to do the right thing, like listening to how his day had gone. She couldn't be bothered to give anything of herself, to plan the future with him that he longed for.

Even her yoga sessions, being with her friends, all the things that she had treasured, became empty. She thought constantly of her parents, of her father, and each day made her more bitter and introspective. So she went out less and less to socialise. Cinemas, the theatre, dinner parties – all receded into memory.

Then Esmine had gone to stay with Janet, albeit temporarily, and Joy was glad that she now had time to herself. She was at least spared the questioning looks, having to explain, to put on a face. It was hard enough doing that eight hours a day.

Lee suggested trips abroad. So they spent weekends in Paris, went to Florence, took short breaks in the Lake District, the Cotswolds, Cambridgeshire. But each served only to accentuate Joy's detachment, highlighting the emptiness that her life had become.

She remembered the times she had wasted when her parents were alive, reproached herself for spoiling those days by quarrelling with them when she could have made those last few weeks happy. If only she had known.

And then it came to her. There was no need to stay in England, nothing that she couldn't lose. She *would* go to Jamaica.

She got out of bed and faced her dark, slender frame in the long pine mirror. She waited. There was nothing this time. No nagging memory of hard boots piercing her skin. No echoes of that terrible pain.

The ceaseless internal pain that had been with her since her parents' death had gone too. She felt incredibly light.

Turning, she caught sight of a full length picture of Esmine over the fireplace. She picked it up and sat on the side of the bed. Oh God, Esmine, how am I going to convince you that I have to go?

It was weeks before Joy could pluck up the courage to talk to her sister. Eventually, one Saturday evening, she suggested that they go out, something they had not done for ages. Esmine left Janet alone for once, and the sisters saw a film in London and then went to Chinatown to eat. Joy was more garrulous than usual but each time she opened her mouth to relay her decision some other topic of conversation came out.

On their way home Joy convinced herself that it wouldn't have been right anyway – their parents had only ever talked about important things at home.

Back at the house she stood watching Esmine making tea for them, her tension at a peak.

Without looking up from the cups, Esmine said dryly, 'Joy, how long are you going to keep me in suspense? It's obvious that you have something on you mind.'

Joy's heart missed a beat.

'Well?'

'I do have something to tell you but let's sit down first.' Her courage failed her. 'Do you want a piece of carrot cake? I made it yesterday.' She tried again to steady her voice but it still came out sounding like somebody else's.

Esmine's eyes were fixed on her. 'Okay. Just a small piece, thanks.'

Joy felt her sister's thoughtful gaze on her. She shuddered as she handed her the cake. She needed to move, to leave the heaviness in the kitchen. 'Let's go into the sitting room, Esmine.'

They sat down side by side, the heaviness lingering. She sipped her tea, staring ahead. Everything seemed out of focus, the prints, the fireplace. Everything! Finally, unable to ignore Esmine's determined eyes, Joy forced herself to meet them.

'Esmine,' Joy stopped, distracted by the anxiety in her sister's eyes. Esmine just continued to stare at her as if she was expecting bad news. Joy looked away, her thumb moving across the raised scar under her chin. 'I've decided to go back . . .'

Esmine continued to look at her then looked away, shaking her head as her mother would have done.

The silence was worse than anything Esmine could have said.

Esmine pursed her lips and took a sip of her tea.

Joy couldn't stand it any more. 'Aren't you going to say anything?'

Esmine grunted, 'What do you want me to say?' Her eyes did not meet Joy's.

'Well how do you feel about it? What do you think?'

Esmine sat up and rested her fingers on her chin.

'Esmine say something!'

Esmine turned and faced her, 'Like what?'

Joy sighed, the corner of her mouth turning up, 'For God's sake Esmine, don't make this more difficult for me than it already is.'

Esmine's voice was calm when she spoke, hiding her disbelief, 'I don't know why you are making this big thing about telling me. My opinion doesn't come into it as you very well know Joy . . .'

'Esmine that's not true . . .'

Esmine shook her head and turned away, 'From the time Mummy and Daddy died Joy, you have been planning it. I'm not stupid.' She lowered her voice, 'Actually, if you really want to know, I'm relieved . . .'

'What?' she shouted. She didn't believe her.

Esmine's eyes filled with tears. 'I just knew that one day you were going to tell me that you were going to leave me by myself.'

Joy sighed. *That's all I need.* 'You won't be by yourself Esmine . . . You've got Janet.'

The tears trickled down Esmine's face, 'That's why you've encouraged me to stay there . . . to ease your conscience,' then almost to herself, 'if you've got one.'

Joy sighed.

Esmine wiped her face with the back of her hand, 'I don't know why, but since that day everything's gone wrong for me . . .'

85

'Esmine, it's not just for you.'

Esmine ignored her, 'One morning I woke up and said goodbye to my parents and the next time I saw them they were lying in the mortuary. Dead! Then those . . . those . . . *men* tried to kill you . . .'

'Oh Esmine, please . . .' She made to hold her but her hands were heavy and she couldn't move them. She didn't want to be blackmailed by tears. She'd had a whole year of her sister's tears and she could take them no more.

Joy closed her eyes and opened them again slowly, the memory bringing the familiar tightness to her face. Her thumb went up to the scar under her chin.

Esmine licked the tears as they ran into her mouth, '. . . And now you are telling me that you are going to leave us . . . leave me alone. How much of all this am I supposed to bear? When is it all going to stop?' She sighed and bit her lips.

Joy forced herself; she rested her hand on her sister's lap. Esmine didn't seem to notice. 'Esmine. Please try to understand why I have to go back. It's no use trying to fool myself. This place can never be home for me. Especially now.'

Esmine looked past her and got up to take a tissue from a box on the magazine rack. When she sat down and spoke again it was as if to someone else in another place. 'It's what Daddy used to say all the time.'

A powerful string pulled at Joy's heart at the mention of her father. It drained and weakened her.

'You've always puzzled me you know, Joy . . . I've never understood you. Never.' Esmine stopped and looked deeply into Joy's face.

'I see,' Joy couldn't think of what else to say.

'. . . Not like the rest of us mere mortals. You were always convinced that everyone loved you and wanted you. That you were everyone's favourite . . . That everything revolved around you and if it didn't then it should . . .'

Joy cocked her head to one side, listening but lost, not knowing how what Esmine was saying was a response to what she had said. She sighed. She had tried so hard in the past year to avoid any discussion about her parents. She had refused to acknowledge Esmine's silent tears. She had ignored all the pain she knew her sister was trying to get out of her system. Now Joy knew she couldn't get away without listening.

'I used to say to myself, how comes everyone says I'm the beautiful one and yet you were the most popular?'

Joy raised her eyebrows.

'I resented you sometimes – your friends, your popularity. The way Daddy loved you best . . .'

'Esmine . . .'

'Joy, let me finish. For once.'

Joy rubbed her fingers over her closed lids.

'I used to find myself wanting you to go to that wretched Jamaica.'

Joy sighed and shifted in her seat.

Esmine ignored her sister's obvious irritation, '. . . in those days when you and him used to spend evening after evening going on about the smell of the land and dead people's graves . . .' she grunted and shook her head, '. . . I used to wish that both of you would just go and leave me some space. Some space to find me . . .' Esmine stopped and focused on a picture of her parents as a young couple, her father's arms fixed around her mother's slender upright shoulders. Her eyes filled up with tears again and she lost their faces under the mist.

Joy waited.

'Now? Now I would give anything to have them . . . him, back. I would give everything to hear his foolish dreams from his own lips.'

Esmine's sobbing brought back memories of the funeral to Joy. The hopelessness she had felt watching the earth scattered on to the coffins. She wanted to get up and leave the room.

Esmine wasn't finished. 'Now that it's only us two left, with them gone, Uncle Lenford and Aunt Sarah gone to America, we only have each other. I just know that I cannot be here by myself. I can't be expected to stay by myself Joy.'

Joy tried to hold her.

Esmine pulled herself away. 'Mummy told you that we had to stay together as a family Joy, so how could you go against her last wish? Why are you so heartless?'

'What about what Daddy wanted?' She couldn't let her have it all her way.

'Joy, don't.' Esmine turned with a frown to her sister. 'Don't try and make it sound as if they died disagreeing. You know that Daddy came round. He accepted what Mummy wanted.'

Joy swallowed, 'Okay Esmine, let's leave it.'

'I don't want to leave it because I don't want you to give the impression to anyone that they died disagreeing.'

'Esmine, I said I don't want to discuss it.'

'Typical. Always your answer if you can't have your own way.' Esmine pouted.

Joy sipped her tea and glanced up at the clock. It was nearly midnight. She was intensely frustrated by the way this talk had gone.

Esmine was persistent. 'You have never really thought for yourself about this Jamaica business, have you Joy?'

'Oh God, Esmine! When are you going to stop fooling yourself?' Joy shouted, 'I've had enough of your whingeing.'

'Call it what you like. It's about time you faced facts. You always try to convince everyone by that exterior of yours that you are in control, that you make your own decisions, that you are independent and free thinking, that you are strong. But it's all a joke. A big joke!' She folded her arms, 'You are really weak. You can't cope here. You haven't got the guts to *fight*, as you would put it, so you want to run away. That's what cowards do.' She stopped and faced Joy, waiting for her to lash out.

Joy met her eyes but said nothing.

Esmine calmed her voice and sighed, 'I'm *trying* to understand . . .'

Joy managed a smile. 'It did start with Daddy.' The smile
widened because she found it impossible to mention him without
smiling. 'But I have developed. I see things with my own eyes now.
It just happens to be what he saw too.'

Esmine shook her head. 'That's convenient.'

Joy got up and stretched. 'I'm tired. I'm going to bed.' She didn't
want to get angry.

'So that's the end of the discussion?'

'We're going round in circles, and you're not interested in
listening to me.'

Esmine didn't get up.

'Come on, you'd better go. It's late.'

Esmine sighed. 'So when are you going?'

Joy sat back down. 'In about a year.'

'Oh! I see. I thought . . .'

'It will take about that time to get everything ready . . .'

'Have you told Lee yet?'

'No. Not yet.' Joy made a face.

'When are you going to tell him?'

'Don't know. I haven't decided yet.'

'What?' Esmine turned to her with a frown.

'Oh no!'

'What?'

'I just remembered. He's supposed to be coming round.'

'And?'

'I just don't feel like seeing him again.'

'Poor Lee . . . Poor me!'

Joy sucked her teeth, 'Oh God, Esmine! Don't burden me.'

Esmine folded her arms and sat back, 'So that's what I am? A burden?'

'I don't meant that.' She closed her eyes.

'If you're tired, go to sleep Joy. I'll go.'

'No!' She stopped and looked at her sister, registering the hurt expression on Esmine's face. 'Look, why don't you stay? We can talk some more. We won't argue. Promise. We can't leave things like this.'

Esmine shrugged.

'You call Janet and I'll call Lee.'

Janet, of course, was sweet. Joy knew that Lee would be less so. As she dialled she found herself, for the second time that day, rehearsing what she was going to say. She understood, not for the first time, what her father meant when he used to speak of doing something with a heavy heart.

As she expected, Lee wasn't at all happy. He said he could have gone to bed or gone out but had stayed up waiting for her to come back from enjoying herself, 'Waiting for permission to see you.'

'I'm sorry baby . . .'

'Joy you know I haven't seen you for ages. You are always doing this!'

'Lee, for God's sake! I need to speak to my sister.'

He inhaled deeply.

She could see him. His dark eyes growing even darker with practised patience, his teeth curling around his heart-shaped lips. 'I know I'm a pain but I have to talk to my sister about something. If you come tomorrow we'll have the whole day together.'

'When am I going to stop taking second place to that sister of yours? To your whims?' He laughed softly but she knew he was hurt. She felt her body tighten with that familiar mix of guilt and irritation.

'Oh Lee, give that a rest. I don't want a quarrel on the phone.'

He sighed loudly.

Joy tried to soften her tone, 'Sweetheart, at least tomorrow I'll be all yours.'

'And there was me thinking that you always holding something back . . .'

Joy sighed heavily, 'Tomorrow then?'

'I had planned to see some people but, as you know, I will change anything for you.'

'Please Lee I *have* apologised already.'

'Okay, okay.'

'See you tomorrow then. About twelve?' She put the phone down and stood for some time, composing herself before going back to Esmine.

But when she got to the bedroom Esmine was on the bed, curled up on her side, as fast asleep as if nothing of importance remained to be said.

Ten

The following morning Esmine opened her eyes and stretched. 'Joy! Joy! What time are you supposed to be meeting Lee?'

'What time is it now?' Joy pressed her eyelids together and yawned. 'I'm so tired . . . I think I'll call him and tell him to meet me tomorrow after work.' She turned on her other side.

'That would be really unfair.' Esmine sprung out of bed and pulled the covers off her sister. 'And I know who he'll blame for that. Me! So get up. It's gone ten.'

Joy curled up, 'Esmine! God. Don't. I'm so tired.'

'Me too. And unlike some I won't be back in bed until tonight.'

Joy opened her eyes and laughed, 'You dirty girl. Anyway, if I'm back in bed it certainly won't be to sleep.'

'Who's the dirty one now? Just get up.' Esmine reached down and yanked her out of bed.

'Oh gee, I hate waking up like this. You really are cruel.' She tried to get back into bed.

Esmine stood between Joy and the bed, arms akimbo.

'Okay. You win.' Joy held up her hands in surrender.

Esmine sat on the side of the bed. 'Joy?'

'Ummm?'

'I think I'll come back home next weekend. We haven't got a lot of time left and we didn't get things sorted last night.'

'I'm not going to die you know baby.' Joy bent and kissed her on the head.

'Oh, *Joy*!'

Joy sat down next to her, 'All right, all right. But what will you do about Janet?'

Esmine paused, 'Well . . . look . . . would you mind if she stayed with us for a while?'

Joy hesitated, 'Oh!'

'Do you mind?'

'Is she well enough . . . I mean . . .'

'Joy! She's just a bit depressed. That's all.'

'Depressed for what is it? A year?'

'Most of the time she's been all right . . .'

Joy sighed and stood up, 'If you like.'

'Joy, I won't ask her if you mind. I don't want her to feel . . .'

Joy nodded, 'It's fine!, It's fine!'

When Esmine left Joy exercised and showered. Despite her frustration with Esmine, she felt excited. There would be no going back, she knew. She had made the decision.

She found herself pacing the room as she waited for Lee. She had feared telling Esmine more than telling him, but now she was not so sure. She decided to employ a strategy she knew never failed to work: seduction. She would get him mellow and then she would spit it out.

She put on her white track-suit and a purple T-shirt. She undid her plaits, pulled her hair tightly back and tied it with a purple lace ribbon. *I must say, Joy Brown, you are a delicious specimen*. Then, with a smile, *You wish*.

Unable to sit still, she browsed through one of the cases she was dealing with at work. She couldn't concentrate so she set it aside. She made herself camomile tea, thinking all the time that she had only herself to blame. She prided herself in being decisive, knowing what she wanted, sticking to her decisions.

But with Lee she had allowed things to slide. Apart from knowing for certain that she didn't want to marry, she didn't always know what she *did* want. There were times when she wanted so much to be free from him. At other times, she couldn't imagine life without him.

Joy drained her cup and got up to make herself another. Six years was a long time – she cleared her throat, apart from occasional dabbles – to be with one man. She had always vowed that she would never be so trapped.

But the thought of seeing him with somebody else made Joy feel murderously jealous and she often wondered whether that was why she held on despite herself.

Joy responded immediately to the rap on the door. In the hall mirror she smiled apprehensively at herself. She opened the door, cocked her head to one side and gave Lee her most winning smile.

He responded beautifully, shining his even white teeth at her, then bit her lightly on the lips and on the neck.

Oh God, she thought, a temor passing through her. Not yet.

'Come in.'

'Thanks for making the time to see me.'

Joy ignored the dig and led him by the hand into the sitting room. Today she had to be in control. Everything would have to be on her terms.

He sat down and crossed his legs, making a triangle in the space between them.

Joy licked her lips. She hadn't realised how hungry she was for him. She had forgotten! That was another reason why she stayed.

'Is Esmine, your only true love, not here then?'

'No, Esmine is not here.' She traced his thighs with her eyes before raising her eyes to meet his.

He smiled at her. 'You look absolutely divine, as usual.'

She rubbed her legs against his thighs. 'Thanks. You don't look too bad yourself.'

He rested his hand around her shoulder. 'So what was so important for you to talk to your sister about then? You made me feel so wanted.' He squeezed her shoulder.

She raised her eyes to the ceiling and sighed, 'Lee I've said it was nothing personal. I just had to speak to her.'

'You told me that but you haven't said what it was about. That is what I am asking.' He took his hand away.

'You asked nothing of the kind.'

'I did. I just did.'

She moved away from him so that their legs were no longer touching.

'Joy, don't be so childish.'

'Lee, don't talk to me like that, you know I don't like it.' She folded her arms.

'But you're not listening to me honey.' His voice changed and she liked the sound of it. More than that she liked the fingers that he was just barely running over her legs.

She shifted back next to him and ran her own fingers over his face and down his neck. He relaxed back into the seat and she climbed into his lap.

'Let's not get into a quarrel sweetheart. I want you now. If you want a row, leave it until later, then I'll give you something to quarrel about.' She buried her lips into his neck and she felt him respond to her.

'You were full of promises on the phone yesterday . . .' He bit her ears as he spoke. He laughed into her ear.

She giggled and moved her lips lightly over his neck.

'Don't disappoint me.' He shifted so that their lips met.

'Have I ever?' She spoke into his mouth.

They slid on to the floor.

'Joy.' He raised himself above her.

'I had planned . . . that . . . we would have . . . a bath . . . I have just the thing for it,' she punctuated her words with nibbles on his ears,

95

bites to his lips, his tongue. 'Then I can give you a massage and then
. . . we can . . . can . . .'

'Let's leave the bath for a while honey. You smell so fresh . . .
You are all I need now . . . afterwards not now . . .'

At university she had noticed him on the first day. She knew he had
noticed her too. As was her practice when she knew she wanted
someone, she had held his eyes just long enough for him to realise
what her intentions were.

At the Black Society Group meetings she had gone to hear him
give a talk on Pan-Africanism.

It was not just that he reminded her of her father or that he spoke
with fire and eloquence, it was mostly, in fact, because he seemed
so unlike her boyfriend of the moment, who spent most of his time
trying to show her that he, not her, was in charge. *His* power games
were wearing her out and she needed a change.

When Lee spoke of the rape of Africa by the Europeans, the
systematic exploitation of Africans and their land, the depletion of
its natural resources by foreign multinationals, it was as if she was
hearing it all for the first time. He quoted Kwame Nkrumah,
Amicar Cabral, Sokoa Toare and Patrice Lamumba. He had ended
with the words, *We want unity, but we need African unity*.

At that time she could not have conceived of him changing or the
fire behind those words ever dying, nor had she dreamt that soon
afterwards he would be building a career as an accountant.

Joy untangled herself from Lee, satisfied. 'God you are beautiful.'

He laughed, 'You always say that afterwards.'

'I'll go up and set the bath then.' She opened the door.

'Back to business then, is it?' He smiled ruefully and she felt the
familiar irritation descend.

'Lee . . .'

'So,' he interrupted her. 'You've decided.'

'What?'

'You've decided that you'll marry me after all. That's what you were telling your sister.'

Joy frowned. 'For God's sake,' she had not meant to raise her voice. She knew it was his idea of a light-hearted way of bringing up the issue of marriage again, but she wasn't amused. 'Why do you always have to be so self-centred Lee? The world does not revolve around you, you know.' Her eyes widened. 'There are times, if you can actually bring yourself to believe it, when you are not the subject of my every thought and conversation.'

Stung by her vehemance, he stepped back, 'Okay, calm down. You don't have to bark at me . . . Christ I don't believe this.'

'Don't believe what?'

'You are so damned self-righteous. I don't know why I'm so foolish. I should know by now that you don't care one iota about me.'

Joy creased her forehead. 'What the hell are you talking about?'

'One minute we're relaxed and having a good time, the next minute you're flying off the handle. You're so unpredictable.'

'Oh yes, it's me is it? If you would only stop and try to see the world outside your narrow perspective then we might get somewhere in this relationship.'

'Get somewhere?' He moved away from the door. '*I'm* the only one who's been trying to get somewhere in this relationship.'

'Oh God!' She moved over to the door and rested her hand on the handle.

'You know it's true.'

'To you getting somewhere means my saying yes to your damned proposal and settling down and having your poxy kids . . .'

'They would be yours too. And what is so wrong with marrying and having kids anyway? Most normal women want to have kids.'

Joy looked at him with scorn and took a deep breath before she spoke. 'You've had your say . . . I'll have mine.' She jabbed the air with her finger, 'I am going to talk about *you*! I know what you've been playing at. It's not me you want. You find it hard to relate to me. You always have done. It's not my fault so don't blame me!' She rested her back on the door to steady herself. Her legs were shaking. 'It's your problem. So own it! You think a woman is only normal if she gives up everything, her identity, her thoughts, herself. Marries and has kids. Well you can stuff that for a start!' She caught her breath but got in again as he opened his mouth. '*I* am not like that. I will never be like that so you can give up trying to get me to conform to your warped standards by trying to make me feel a freak!'

'You said it sweetheart.' He turned his back to her for a moment.

Joy's anger was such that all she could do to contain herself was to leave him. She went into the hall. She wanted to stop now and do as he had done, to apologise and take up where they had left off, but she knew she couldn't.

He came after her.

She swung round and faced him, 'Tell me something Lee. When are you going to stop deluding yourself into believing that you hold the key to my happiness?' Without giving him the chance to answer she continued. 'You talk like someone who's trapped in a dream, or should I say a nightmare? I am wide awake baby and I know what I'm talking about. You clearly don't.'

'That's you all over isn't it?' He stuffed his hands into his pockets. 'As soon as you start to lose an argument you start insulting me. I am not going to stay here and listen to your rubbish. You and you damned sister can go to hell. Who needs you?'

If there was anything she hated, it was him dragging Esmine into their arguments.

He knew it but could not resist it.

'Listen, get the hell out of our house! Don't you dare drag my sister into this, or use her to get at me. Perhaps you should try and work out your own relationship with your own family. Get out of our house!'

'Darling, I'm sorry . . .' He took his hand out of his pocket and reached for her.

'Don't you darling me. Just get the hell out of my life.' She strode up to the front door and flung it open.

He followed her, pleading with her with his eyes and trying to hold her.

She knocked away his arms, 'Just get out!'

'Joy, please.'

'I said get out! Get the hell out of my life.'

He stepped outside and dropped his shoulders, sighing.

She slammed the door behind him.

Eleven

The phone rang at last.

Joy jumped to get it but stopped herself just in time. She must be calm. She mustn't appear too anxious to forgive. She would let him suffer for a while. Let him beg.

Her heart sank. It wasn't Lee. It was one of Esmine's friends. Joy spoke to her, trying to hide the bitter disappointment in her voice.

Afterwards she held the receiver for a moment before putting it down. So he was not going to call? She had given him time to get home. To calm down. She had sat by the phone all afternoon, something she would never admit to anyone, waiting for his call. She couldn't believe it as the minutes ticked into hours and the phone remained silent.

She went over and over in her mind what had happened. What he had said. What she had said. The exact tone of his voice. His insinuations. His cheek. His blasted cheek. His bloody cheek!

Perhaps it *was* best that he hadn't called. Her lips tightened again, her breathing coming in quick gasps.

She decided to take a walk. Striding down the street furiously, she thought: 'If he calls, fine, if he doesn't then he can really go to hell this time. Who needs him?' She only realised she had spoken out loud when the couple passing her sniggered. She shrugged her shoulders and strutted past them.

Back home she turned on the television just for the background noise. What on earth had come over Lee? They had had worse rows before. He had always called, always begged her forgiveness. He had never taken so long before.

In between cups of tea, switching the television on and off, she called her sister. Eventually she got through. 'Where have you been? I've been calling you all evening.'

'I didn't think you'd have the time to call me. What's up?'

Joy grunted, 'Was Janet all right?'

'Yes, she's fine. I suppose I needn't ask if Lee is all right?'

Joy didn't reply.

'Did you hear what I said?'

'What?'

'What's wrong with you Joy? Are you listening or what?'

'Sorry. What did you say?'

'I said, is Lee exhausted?' Esmine giggled.

'God knows. He's not here.'

'Oh, it's only . . .'

'We had a massive row.'

'I see. What did you do?'

'What do you mean what did *I* do? Why must it be me?'

'Okay Joy, calm down.' There was a pause. 'What happened then?'

Joy sighed, 'I suppose it was me . . . Quite frankly I was beastly but he should understand me by now, and anyway he said some pretty nasty things.'

'I bet you gave as good as you got though?'

'Esmine, it's not a joke. It's serious this time. He hasn't called . . .'

'I see . . . It *is* serious.'

'Oh Essy. I *want* him to call.'

'Call him . . .'

'No!'

'Joy don't cut off your nose to spite your face.'

'I don't care. I won't call him. If he wants me let him call.'

Neither of them spoke for sometime. 'If he wants me he'll have to take me as I am. If he can't then he doesn't deserve me.'

'You do bite you know. I pity Lee.'

'That's loyalty for you. My one and only sister taking sides against me.' Joy was wounded.

'I'm not. I don't mean to.'

'Really?' Her voice was impatient.

'Anyway, Cheer up.'

'I'm all right.'

'Joy you don't always have to play tough you know.'

'Thank you Esmine. I've had enough lectures today to last me a life time. I don't need any more. I'm all right. Hear from you tomorrow. Love you.'

'Me too. Bye.'

She was not all right. She made to pick up the phone several times but her hand rested heavily over the receiver and she had to withdraw. The more depressed she felt, the more her mind sifted and found reasons for even greater unease.

Her thoughts finally rested on one of the more persistent of Lee's admirers. What was her name? Joy went through all the letters of the alphabet and tried to think of names beginning with each letter. It wouldn't come.

When she had first met her she had had one of her most serious rows with Lee.

She had gone to his home for dinner, and there was his sister, Grace, who she had always disliked, with a friend of hers. Joy disliked her on sight. For a start, the woman had monopolised the conversation at dinner.

She had begun, 'Lee, do you remember how infatuated you were with me when we were in the sixth form?' She pushed her already ample chest towards him. He had looked across the table at Joy and tried to smile.

'Do you remember you used to call me the Queen of Sheba?'

Joy rested back in her chair and would have burst out laughing if she had not felt the anger rising in her.

'A lot of girls used to be jealous of me you know. Do you remember Lee? You see my hair has always been long. I have good hair, I don't need to press it ... When I went to the West Indies for the first time people were always asking me if I was mixed.' She smiled, meeting the eyes of Lee's parents.

Joy was overcome with the urge to say, *mixed up, you mean*, but shook her head instead.

'Remember how you used to love running your hands through it? You always said how naturally soft it was.' She smoothed her hair back. Grace cleared her throat, looked from the top of Lee's head to Joy's forehead. She carefully avoided Joy's eyes.

'I didn't like Lee at first,' she turned and looked across the table at Joy.

Their eyes met.

It was as if she had tried to look directly into the sun. She squinted and averted her gaze but continued. 'He was so persistent though, so in the end I gave in ... My friends kept saying how lucky I was. The best looking guys always went after me you see.'

'It just goes to show, doesn't it?' Joy couldn't resist saying.

'Joy darling, this is the way you like you fish isn't it?' Lee interrupted, rather desperately.

Joy's eyes flared. The woman rambled on.

'They all liked you, didn't they Lee? And I used to say to them, it wasn't my fault that you had eyes only for me.' She rested her hand on Lee's arm and smiled into his face.

'You are one girl who like to hear the sound of her own voice,' Lee's father commented, his eyes still on his plate.

It didn't help; it only made Joy even more furious. She didn't want his pity. What she wanted was just one minute alone with Lee.

'Oh, I hope I'm not spilling any beans. Anyway, about what you

103

said about me speaking a lot. My father used to say that. But in my job, as a personnel officer, I need to.' She pushed her chest out, 'Anyway most people like the way I speak . . . You see I had elocution lessons when I was at school.' She looked around the table with a self-satisfied grin but carefully avoided Joy's eyes.

Joy rested her knife and fork on her plate.

Lee saw the signs – pouted lips, the frown – incongruous on her unlined forehead. She lifted her head and slowly raised her chin.

He got in before her, 'Darling?'

She turned him a slanted look of utter disdain.

He swallowed hard.

'Lee, do you remember how you used to like my cooking?' The woman was oblivious of the mounting tension.

Joy stared at Lee. She couldn't believe he wasn't doing anything! He looked at his sister, Grace. Joy was sure he wanted her to stop the woman for him. At least that was something. She shifted in her seat, relishing his discomfort.

Grace shrugged and continued eating. Joy could swear she had a smile on her face.

Without warning, the woman turned the conversation to Joy. 'I hear Joy that you insist on Lee sharing the cooking with you.' Although she spoke to Joy she still did not look at her. 'I believe that there are certain things that a woman is best at . . . I certainly like looking after the man I'm going with. And all this healthy eating stuff . . . I'm not into it at all. You know, Lee, when we were talking about it the other day, when you said that Joy was obsessed with her body . . .'

Joy was furious. She shot him her most vicious stare yet. If only his parents weren't there.

'What? I didn't say that . . .' He coughed, trying to dislodge the rice that had gone down the wrong way.

'Don't you remember? You know: when I said that personally I thought that a woman is more attractive with some flesh on her body. I think that women who have all this muscle and no breasts look unnatural. They look like men.' She looked across at Joy, somewhere from her chin down.

'I didn't say that Joy is obsessed. I never said anything of the sort.'

'I could have sworn you did . . . Well perhaps not the exact words but something like that . . . Oh, I hope I'm not saying too much. I don't want to get you into trouble. I know that you are really under heavy manners these days.' She smiled and rested her arm around his shoulder.

Joy rested her elbow on the table. Lee was still avoiding her eyes. This was too much for her. She had to speak.

'I wish you'd shut up!' she shouted, her eyes firmly fixed on the woman.

All eyes shot in her direction.

Lee looked furtively round the table.

Joy didn't care what he was doing. 'If you two want to be alone to continue your conversation, why don't you leave the table? You're giving me indigestion.' The woman withdrew her arm from Lee's shoulders as Joy's cold contempt made itself felt.

Lee choked on the rice, cleared his throat but got no sympathy.

Joy ignored him. 'If you don't mind, save all this until you're in private with Lee. This is clearly for *his* benefit.' Her hands were trembling with fury.

'You certainly have an old head on that young body of yours,' Lee's mother said, reaching out and patting Joy's arm. She got up, 'I have some carrot juice in the kitchen. I'll get it. Grace, help me clear the table.'

Joy watched as Grace and her friend shuffled from their chairs and scrambled to take plates from the table. She was exhausted with anger. She tapped the floor in an attempt to discharge some of it. Blasted cheek. Just wait! She glared at Lee. But he wouldn't meet her eyes.

Eventually, he reached across the table to take her free hand. She slipped her hand off the table, wiping the tentative smile off his face.

As soon as the table was cleared, she got up and thanked his mother. So what if it was rude to eat and then leave at once?

'Going already dear?' she asked.

'Yes. I'm sorry. I have some work to do.'

'Okay dear. See you again soon,' Lee's mother said.

Joy said goodbye to Lee's father but did not spare a glance for Grace or her friend.

'I'll come with you.' Lee joined her in the hallway.

'No!' Then more dispassionately, 'No. You stay and finish your conversation about me with your friend. You . . .'

The dining room door suddenly opened and Joy turned to see the woman behind them, 'Goodbye Joy . . . Lee can you give me a lift home later please? It will be too late to take the tube by the time I'm ready to go.'

Joy looked at him and shook her head before opening the front door, leaving him standing open mouthed in the hall.

Her hand shook as she searched for her car keys. She didn't really believe that he had discussed her with anyone, let alone that . . . that thing, but God he was so *pathetic*! Why hadn't he shut the stupid woman up?

Joy got up, still unable to remember the woman's name.

She hadn't eaten all day. She exercised, showered and fixed a salad. She sat and picked at it before covering it and putting it into the fridge. No more phone calls came that day. She didn't work, and with each passing moment she hated herself more for letting him spoil her weekend.

That night she listened to an album, one that normally made her prance and jump around the room. It did nothing for her, so at well past midnight she went to bed.

That week, on the surface, Joy was her usual self. Only Esmine knew she was miserable, and feared secretly that Lee and her sister had finally finished.

On Friday, after work, Joy went to her florist to collect her usual order. It was there that she made the decision. She asked for a bunch of roses to be sent to Lee's address.

'Sure. Which ones would you like? There's red, white . . .'

Joy looked sceptically at the bunches of flowers on the floor in front of her. 'Ten red ones I suppose,' she said without enthusiasm.

She sighed, pushing her fermenting anger to the back of her mind. She had decided that there was no way she'd let it end like that – not when she was still in the country, not until *she* was good and ready. Yet she knew if she thought too much about what he'd said, and the fact that he hadn't called, she'd cancel and walk out of the shop. She handed the florist the address.

'Would you like a message on the card dear?'

Joy thought for a moment, 'Yes. I'll write it thanks.'

She scribbled, *If you still want me as much as I want you, call. Please. J.* She handed the card to the florist.

'A little tiff with your young man?'

'It was rather a big one actually.'

The woman smiled at Joy, 'This should do the trick.'

Joy picked up her briefcase, 'I hope so.'

She walked out of the shop, her heart a little lighter than it had been all week, but more than a little resentful.

Twelve

The following day Joy woke to a heavy thumping on the door. Before she knew where she was she was half-way down the stairs. She glanced at the clock in the hallway as she struggled to get her dressing gown on. It was eleven o'clock. She hated being woken in this way.

She caught sight of herself in the mirror as she tied the string of her gown. Goodness! What a sight. How could I have slept so late?

'Who is it?' she called as she undid the bottom bolt. There was no reply.

'I said who is it?'

She pulled back the door to face Lee on the doorstep.

He smiled tentatively.

'Oh no, not you . . .'

'Oh!' He took a step back, his hands stuffed in his pockets, and bit on his bottom lip. At other times the sight of his even white teeth and his top lip shaped like a heart would have sent her hands reaching to trace the lines.

'I thought with the red roses and . . .'

'I didn't meant that. I meant look at the state of me . . . You woke me up . . . I mean I overslept . . . It's late . . . Oh come in.'

She led the way into the sitting room, conscious of her hair sticking up on end, her unwashed face, her unbrushed teeth, her threadbare dressing gown.

Before she sat down she stole a glance at him. *God he's beautiful. I wish I could jump all the nonsense and grab hold of him.*

He sat down next to her but no part of their bodies touched. They might have been meeting for the first time. She hadn't planned it that way when she had spent all those empty evenings hoping he'd call.

'Thanks for the roses. They're beautiful.'

He was staring at her.

She was avoiding his eyes.

'Joy, I've missed you . . .'

The intensity in his voice startled her.

'I'm sorry . . .'

'You don't have to apologise.' The words barely came out.

'Joy, let me finish.' But he said nothing else.

'I really must shower.' She stood up. He stood up too. Instead of turning, she walked towards him and enfolded her arms around him. She moved one of her arms to rest on his neck and ran the other up and down his back.

He relaxed as she tightened her arms around him.

They pulled apart and looked at each other. She held him again, caressed his whole body, his head, his ears, his face, his back. She kissed his face, licking his mouth, bit his heart-shaped lips until she knew he was ready for her.

Then she pulled him down on the settee and then on to the floor. Their lips met, becoming one, the same teeth, the same tongue, the same body.

'I've missed you.'

'Me too.'

Their clothes lay crumpled in the corner of the pine bathroom floor. They were luxuriating in the hot, soft water, topping it up as the temperature dropped.

'This is so nice,' Lee whispered, his lips touching her ears.

'Ummm . . .' she responded, her back pressing into his chest and stomach. She could feel the soft damp hair on his chest, like grass in the fresh morning dew. The back of her head relaxed on to his shoulder as she massaged his thighs, his legs, his knees under the water.

He pulled his legs down and entwined their toes.

She turned, sat back on her heels, bent forward and covered his face with wet kisses. She ran her hands over his body, slowly.

She played with his ears, his lips, his fingers, his eyes.

'You have the most amazing body darling.' He breathed the words into her ears. 'It's so dark, firm, not one ounce of fat, so well defined, so proportioned. I love it, touching it, feeling it. I dream of it at nights.'

Joy giggled, throwing her head back. 'You make me tingle. Yours. Your body. Well let me tell you about it. It's the best. You have everything. I love the hair, it's so soft. I love the colour, jet black. Like polished ebony. You are like a rock, hewn from the only stone of its kind. I love your body. It does all kinds of things to me. I love it. I love you. I want to eat you up.'

She bit his cheeks, his mouth, his chest, again and again, and as he writhed she blew the softest breath over each area she bit. His neck, his lip; kiss, blow, bite, kiss . . .

'Oh Joy . . . Please spare me. Please . . . I love it . . . darling.'

There was little tension in his back now. Joy used a combination of massage and caresses to smooth the oil into his back. She was astride his back on the bed. She started with his neck, squeezing, rubbing, stroking. Penetrating to the bones. His shoulders, his bottom, thighs, legs. Rubbing, tapping, slapping, stroking . . . She was finding it hard to keep to the task at hand. He was obviously struggling too. He tried to throw her off him, to get up.

'Lie down Lee. I haven't finished yet.' She pushed him back on the bed.

'Oh Joy you are wicked . . . The oil smells wonderful. What is it?'

'My own secret recipe. Isn't it wonderful?'

'Oh Joy, I can't hold on any longer . . .'

'Lee lie down. I haven't finished . . . I'm enjoying this as much as you, if not more, so don't be selfish.'

'You are a wicked woman.' She felt him shudder and went over the same spot again.

'You're torturing me.' Turning sharply, he threw her off balance, catching her as she fell backwards.

Thirteen

Joy and Lee had planned to do fried rice for lunch, only to find that they didn't have any of the key ingredients, like rice. Joy was just about to go in search of a shop when Esmine and Janet arrived.

Joy and her sister hugged and kissed.

Janet stood back, arms folded tightly into her body.

'Hello Janet. Good to see you.' Joy hugged her too.

'It's good to see you Lee.' Esmine threw her arms around him. 'I hope big Sis has been looking after you?'

He straightened his back and found a smile for her, 'As always.'

'Good. We won't intrude for too long.'

He turned his attention to Janet, 'It's good to see you. It's been a long time.' His voice was gentle. 'How are you feeling?'

'Not bad now. Thanks to Esmine.'

'I was just about to go out to find a shop. You hungry?' Joy asked.

'Not particularly but I'll come with you.'

'Okay, come with me to find a shop then Essy. Will you be all right Janet? We won't be long.'

Janet said she'd unpack the few items she had brought with her. 'By the way, thanks a lot Joy,' she said, unfolding her arms and squeezing her fingers together.

'Don't mention it. It's good to have you.'

Lee stuffed his hands in his pockets and went back into the kitchen.

'So, Joy. The flowers worked then?' Esmine said with a cheeky grin, as Joy drove off.

'Yes but I shouldn't have had to send them.'

'Oh Joy!' Esmine shook her head. 'How did he take your news?'

'I haven't told him yet.'

Esmine shouted, '*You haven't*?'

'I thought it would have spoilt it,' she said, immediately regretting her honesty. Esmine would certainly use it against her in the future. She was usually on Lee's side, accusing Joy of being too cynical about the relationship, of using Lee.

Esmine smoothed back her hair and pressed her painted lips together. She flipped the mirror down and examined her face. 'So you are scared?' she asked slowly.

They were waiting at a stop light. 'Of what?' Joy pretended she didn't know what her sister meant.

'Telling Lee of course.'

'Of course not . . . Don't be silly. I would say he's lucky.'

'Of course,' Esmine retorted sarcastically.

Joy sighed, changing gears roughly as she sped away from the lights. 'Well actually, I have come very close to calling it a day . . .'

Esmine tutted, 'You've been saying that for years . . .'

'I meant it this time.'

'What's so different now?'

Joy glanced at her sister, wondering if she dared honesty. *What the hell. She has enough ammunition to use against me already.*

'Go on,' Esmine pressed. 'What's so different about now?' Esmine's eyes widened, 'You haven't got someone . . .'

'No!'

'So why are you going to finish?'

'I said I *was* going to. I've changed my mind.'

Esmine tutted and took a deep breath, 'You are something else

113

you know, Joy.' She eyed Joy angrily, 'So?'

Joy ran her thumb under her chin, 'I suppose the thought of him with someone else while I'm still here . . .'

'You digust me!'

'Take his side as usual.'

'Joy, even you can see what you're doing. You're using the man. That's awful!'

'He's enjoying himself too . . .'

'That's not all relationships are supposed to be about you know Joy.'

'Of course they are. Anyway what do you know about relationships? . . . You spend your whole life running from men. Perhaps when you . . .'

'Just shut up about me! It's you we're talking about.' Esmine shook her head, 'You're a classic case of *I don't want the man but I don't want anybody else to have him.*'

'That's true.' Joy said smugly, amused at having taken the wind out of her sister's sails. That was exactly how she'd wanted to put it to her sister. The smile crept across her lips; it sounded much better coming from Esmine.

'What are you smiling about Joy? You should be ashamed. You just don't have any feeling do you?'

Joy bit her lips, 'You're getting worked up over nothing Esmine. Lee wouldn't thank you. Give him a week after I leave and you'll see him walking down the high street with some other woman.'

They were pulling up outside the shop. Esmine looked seriously at Joy, 'Can't you see that he worships you? I can see it in his eyes . . .' She lowered her voice as if she feared Lee might hear her. 'Eyes tell me a lot, believe me. He watches you all the time. He is always touching you with his eyes.'

'He's always touching me you mean.'

'Lucky you.'

'He's the lucky one.' Joy stopped the car. 'Let's get this food and get back. I suppose I *do* need to get this over and done with.'

'Sis?'

'Yes.' Their brown eyes met.

'Lee can't ever feel it more than I do . . .'

'Oh Esmine. I know . . . I know.' She kissed her sister on the mouth.

'It's a tough life.'

'Lee, honey,' Joy gulped. 'I have decided to go home to Ja.'

The album finished. They were sitting together on the sofa, long after Esmine and Janet had gone to bed. She heard the arm of the turntable swing back to rest. She heard his breathing, her breathing, felt her heart thumping. He didn't reply.

She turned to read his face. There was nothing.

'I'll be going back next year. In November, my father's birthday . . . I don't feel that I belong here. I have to go . . .'

When he spoke he might have been in another room, a room with little air. 'I see.'

'Is that all you are going to say?'

'What else do you want me to say?'

'I don't know. I thought . . .'

'You thought . . .' He nodded his head as he spoke, 'You thought . . . Go on, tell me what you thought.'

Joy visibly sank back into her chair as their eyes finally met. She didn't know what to say she thought.

'This is exactly like you. What you have always been like. Since that day you condescended to go out with me . . .'

'What?' She creased her forehead but she might not have spoken.

'Joy makes decisions, she makes up her mind about things and then she tells me about them. And if I don't happen to like it, then tough. Joy has made up her mind!'

'Lee what are you talking about? We're not discussing the past now'.

'That's what you call a discussion is it?'

'Lee, I'm the only one who can make this decision. It concerns me.'

He turned and faced her again.

She sank back further in her chair.

He raised his voice, 'I don't understand you Joy. So it only concerns you . . . the fact that you are telling me, in your usual ice-cool way, that you have made the decision to destroy what we have of a relationship. So that doesn't concern me?' He shook his head and lowered his voice, 'No discussion, nothing!'

'I'm giving us a chance to discuss it now.'

He laughed scornfully, 'Do me a favour Joy. Don't insult my intelligence – or yours. As usual I've come last.'

'Last? What are you talking about? The only person I've told is Esmine.'

'That's exactly what I mean.'

'For God's sake Lee. Don't start that please. One minute you're upset because I didn't tell you even before I'd decided myself. The next minute you're upset because I told Esmine first. Make up your mind.' She was trying hard to control the irritation that was creeping into her voice, but she was not succeeding.

He got up impatiently to flip over the album, then walked across the room and picked up a picture of her and Esmine that had been resting over the fireplace.

Joy got up and embraced him from behind.

He didn't respond. He replaced the picture, unfolded her arms, turned, walked back to the settee and sat down. She shook her head and followed him.

'Whenever I think that something is at last really happening between us you quickly change my mind. You build me up then smash me down. Last week . . . What? A few hours ago. Oh God why are you so selfish, so cruel, so callous? You are always showing me what a fool I am . . .'

'I don't think you are a fool.' Her voice was soft.

'I must be. Since I met you it has been an uphill struggle.'

He shot her a serious, cutting look.

'All right then, Lee, tell me why it has been such an uphill struggle.'

'I won't waste your time.'

'Lee, don't be such a baby! Anyway it's not that I haven't told you in the past . . . when Daddy was alive . . . what we wanted.'

'Exactly. I wondered when you'd admit it.'

'Admit what?' she said impatiently.

'I thought at the time, when your father was alive, because you were so close . . . that you were just going along with all that to please him.'

'I don't believe it,' she said, angry.

He looked at her, 'I did. I've said as much in the past.'

'Well you were wrong! Weren't you?'

'You don't have to shout Joy. You're so sensitive when anything concerns your father!'

'I'm not. I just don't want you to use his name in vain.'

'Joy we are not talking about God . . .'

'*Lee don't*!'

He drew a deep breath, 'So I can't speak my mind? That is *your* prerogative I suppose?'

'I didn't say that.'

She tried to calm herself but her thumb found her chin.

He reached across and took her hand away. 'Joy please listen to me. You don't have to do this if it's not what you want to do. Your father is dead. He would want you to do what makes you happy.'

'You don't understand Lee. You will never understand.'

'Try me.'

'I *am* doing it for me. But . . . He was so right about this place. All he always said was right. I can't stay here. I have to get out.'

'Why Joy? Why?' He tightened his grip on her hand.

'Where do I begin?' She pulled her hand out of his and raised it again to her chin.

He watched her, 'Was it . . . was it those blokes?' The anger against them rose again. He took her fingers and kissed them.

She sighed. 'That's only part of it. But I suppose they represent what life here is really like . . . They showed me that I'll have to expend too much energy fighting if I'm going to survive. I'll spend my life angry – angry with faceless, nameless people. And once I've spent all that energy fighting, there'll be no time to really live, to be happy.'

'Can't I make you happy?' He leaned forward and kissed her on the chin.

'Lee you know you can. You do.'

'So why are you planning to leave me?'

'You know it's not like that. I'm not leaving you as such.'

'Joy, I would like you to tell me how we can conduct a relationship from five thousand miles apart.'

She sighed and traced his face with her eyes. *God, why does he look so much like my father sometimes?*

He shook his head. 'You know, when I first met you I didn't think you could be for real. You had it all – beauty, strength, independence, brightness, all wrapped up in the same package.' He looked deeply into her face. 'But if I'm honest, the same things I saw and loved in you then, are the very things that are causing me to hurt now.'

'I can't help the way I am. I've always told you there is no point trying to change me.'

'You know I don't want to do that. All I want to do is to try and understand you.'

She didn't reply.

Eventually he spoke, 'So that's us then Joy.' He sounded close to

118

tears. She looked at him, wanting to nod and to shake her head at the same time. She did nothing.

She found instead her father's voice inside her head and it sounded to her like the song of the gentlest of breezes on a hot day. It smoothed back the hair from her face and made her cool despite the heat.

I will tell you this honeybunch . . . You know our national bird is the humming bird? She saw him cock his head to one side and smiling. It is a bird that doesn't sing . . . That's why it's called humming . . . The wings . . . they hummm . . . As a boy they used to fascinate me. I used to get as close as I could and watch it. Its long beak in the flower, its wings making the sweetest of sounds . . . humming . . . humming . . . But hear this! When we take off from this place . . . Believe me honeybunch . . . humming birds . . . will sing for joy . . . They will sing babydear . . .

'What's the matter?' Lee stroked her hand.

'Sorry? What?'

'Your eyes are kind of transparent.'

'Are they? I'm fine.' She snuggled up to him to hide the pleasure that she knew infused her face.

Fourteen

Once Esmine and Lee had been told, a new vitality came over Joy. She was almost her usual self again, hardly ever at home, her work and social diary packed.

Esmine wasn't happy. She accused Joy of pushing her out, of not making time for her. Joy's excuse was that she didn't want to get between her and Janet. When she had said this, it had come out sounding as if she were jealous. Nothing could have been further from the truth.

Although she still didn't really like Janet staying with them, Joy was pleased Esmine had somebody. She knew that Janet felt she needed Esmine. She knew Esmine needed Janet. Whatever the reality, Joy felt eased of her responsibility for her sister. Because of this she endured Janet's presence, careful not to interfere or to make any comment about the situation that had brought her to their house. It wasn't long however before Esmine suggested to Joy that Janet might as well move in completely. Before Joy had the chance to protest Esmine informed her that she had already put the idea to Janet and that she had been overjoyed.

Joy was furious, insisting that Esmine should have discussed it with her first.

'What are you saying?' Esmine was equally annoyed. 'This house is more yours than mine? You're just selfish. There are four bedrooms in this house. Besides, you don't think about me when you make your decisions. You do what pleases you. Just let me do the same!' she had shouted and walked out of the room.

Joy felt bad about it. She felt Esmine had misunderstood her. She didn't have anything personal against Janet, she just couldn't understand why she was so weak. Esmine refused to discuss it again, saying she had made her decision and that if Joy didn't like it, they could sell up and get their own places. Joy hadn't meant it to get to that, and to appease her sister she booked a weekend in a hotel in Sussex just for the two of them. There was no pleasing Esmine; she complained that Joy should have discussed it with her first, succumbing only when Joy said that it had been a credit card booking and that she couldn't get her money back.

Janet said she'd use the weekend to clear out her flat and pack everything ready for Esmine to collect her on the Sunday, oblivious of what had transpired between the sisters.

After the tension of the Friday evening, they settled in and began to enjoy themselves. They walked the Downs, shopped in the Lanes in Brighton, bought antique jewellery, ate hearty pub meals by real log fires.

On the Saturday evening Joy watched from their ample four-poster bed as Esmine applied baby lotion to her body. She was wondering, not for the first time, why Esmine had never had a relationship for any length of time. There had been so many possibilities over the years. Esmine had never taken any of them seriously. 'What a waste eh?' Joy, rolled over on her side, articulating half of her thoughts.

Esmine followed her eyes, 'What?'

'That body of yours.'

Esmine sucked her teeth, 'You're such a contradiction.'

'Why?'

'One minute you go on about looking after yourself for yourself, the next minute you talk this nonsense.'

'I'm only wanting you to know what you're missing.'

'Nothing that can't wait,' Esmine went to brush her teeth.

'You'll regret it,' Joy shouted after her.

Esmine came out of the bathroom in a T-shirt she had bought on their last trip to Jamaica. It promised heaven in the Island of Paradise. 'I suppose that's chosen to mock me?' Joy said frivolously.

Esmine looked down at the words, 'I thought you'd say something about it. Nowhere is paradise, Joy, or anywhere can be paradise. It's all a state of mind.'

Joy knitted her brow. Something in Esmine's tone made her regret speaking. She reached out and took her sister's hand. 'Try not to be so angry. It's nothing personal.'

Esmine withdrew her hand 'What's nothing personal?'

'Leaving, going back.' She couldn't help it, she couldn't go through months of this sniping.

'It doesn't preoccupy me as much as it does you, you know Joy. If you can actually bring yourself to believe that.'

Joy raised her eyes to the ceiling. She sat up, feeling a sudden yearning to have her parents back. She missed her father. She hated facing her sister so totally alone on the topic, with her years of entrenched scepticism and resentment.

Despite their moving house soon after their parents' death Joy could still feel her father's spirit. Not a day passed when she did not turn slowly to look over her shoulder because she felt him behind her. She would feel her hands warm up. She heard him speak. Heard his laugh.

In the hotel there was no such feeling. No assurance.

Esmine sat down by a coffee table on the opposite side of the room, a range of nail polish in front of her. She picked one up to examine the contents next to her nails. She replaced the bottle, turning to Joy. 'Do you think Daddy died weighed down with this thing about being a stranger here? Feeling rootless?'

Joy was taken aback. She thought the subject closed. She had certainly not intended to raise it again this weekend. 'I don't think he was ever weighed down by it Esmine. It was his inspiration.' She had never thought of it like that before, and now that it came out it felt authentic.

'Ummm. You see I don't think it's healthy to burden yourself with all this thing about where we belong and all that. We belong where we want to belong. We belong where we work to build. Nobody can deny that we have all sweated blood to build this place.' She looked sideways at Joy. 'So it's sacrilegious then to throw it all up. To give it all up. To give up our birthright.'

As mummy would say, Joy thought, but said, 'That's where we are different.' She turned fully to face Esmine. 'I don't see it as giving up anything. I see it as gaining. As finding me.'

'You have never struck me as lost.'

Joy shook her head slightly, as her mother would have done. 'Parts of all of us are lost. So lost that we don't even know that those parts ever existed. Our true selves, the selves that control our own lives.'

'I've never lost any part of me. What you are looking for are things that don't exist . . . You create issues and problems that don't exist.' She opened one of the bottles and started to apply the nail polish.

Her nonchalance irritated Joy. 'Esmine if you can't see all the problems, all the hate around you, directed at you, then I honestly give up!' She went under the covers, suddenly feeling cold.

'Joy, *you* are creating problems for yourself. And what hate? If unnamed people hate me, they can only hurt themselves. It doesn't touch me. You should just get on with your life, *stop* taking this whole country on. You'll only lose.'

'That's precisely what I have no intention of doing! That's why I'm getting out.'

'Escaping! Like those who dream of the home in the skies . . .'

'No, like those who dream of freedom and liberation.'

123

'I just fear that you are going to have a very rude awakening when you land in Jamaica and see that freedom doesn't come with the sun and the sea.'

'As Mummy would say.'

'Yes! As Mummy *rightly* said.'

Joy got up out of bed. She opened the curtains and looked out on to the street. The horse-chestnut trees by the window moved only slightly in the autumn breeze. Everything else was still.

Suddenly, Joy realised she too was calm. She was so certain in herself that she was doing the right thing that nothing outside could change it. She turned back to her sister, 'I can't show the world my heart, but if it really wants to see it can look into my eyes. It will see the pains and the scars.' Her fingers went up to her chin.

Esmine didn't reply.

'I can't live and breathe pain and hostility any longer, Essy.'

Esmine sighed and continued painting her nails.

Now that she had started, Joy felt the need to finish. 'You have to understand that I am not advocating what I plan to do for anyone else. What I am going to do is what *I* have to do. It's personal.'

Esmine used her gentlest voice. 'Joy have you stopped to consider that what you plan to do will be a victory for them?'

Joy heard the change in her voice and moved closer to her. Their eyes met.

'People like those animals who . . . who attacked you.'

Joy's face changed. Esmine reached out and took Joy's hand. It was shaking. She raised Joy's fingers to her lips and kissed them.

'I shouldn't have reminded you.'

'I can never forget.' She withdrew her hand gently from her sister's, sat down on the floor and pulled her knees up. Her sigh was long and broken.

'For a lot of reasons I don't ever want to forget.'

'Joy, get back into bed. You're shaking.'

Joy tried to smile but didn't move. 'You know what still frightens me?' Her voice was distant.

Esmine strained her ears. She could hardly hear her.

'I feel now that I can kill! I lie awake sometimes seeing their faces. Hoping that one day I'll see them crossing the road in front of my car and sometimes I feel I would give all I own for that one ultimate satisfaction.'

She raised her arm and rested it on top of Esmine's. 'Do you remember how I looked Esmine? My eyes swollen and half-closed . . . All the blood . . . Stitches and butterflies holding my skin together?'

'Oh Joy!' Esmine got up and held her.

'Do you remember the police in the hospital? When I could hardly talk for shaking with fright and anger, asking me if I was sure they were white? Do you remember?' She got up.

Esmine walked with her over to the bed and sat down with her. 'Joy, you mustn't keep it all in you know. It's not good for you to keep it all in like this . . .'

Joy raised her head and kissed her sister. 'I can't cry Essy. You know I don't find it easy to cry anymore.'

Esmine ran her own fingers across the length of the scar under her sister's chin. Her blood ran cold.

'I'll never get over it.' Joy shuddered, a coldness coming over her.

Esmine hugged her, 'I know.'

'It all happened so quickly.' Joy spoke quietly, 'I thought they were going to kill me . . . At one point I hoped they'd kill me! To stop that awful pain.'

Esmine kissed her repeatedly. It was the first time Joy had spoken about the incident. She had always refused before. 'You kept flashing across my mind . . . I kept thinking how unfair it was that, so soon after Mummy and Daddy, I would die too and leave you all by yourself.' She bit her lips, '. . . I kept feeling my skin opening and the blood running . . . You know how easily my skin scars. Strange isn't it? Faced with death and thinking of my stupid

125

face. You see, all the time I couldn't really tell where they were hitting me. It was everywhere . . . my whole body was hurting . . . I was feeling pain all over me.'

Esmine held her. How she wished their father was there. She knew he would have made it better for Joy.

Taking a deep breath, Joy cuddled up against her sister, 'The doctors did a good job, didn't they? Only the scar here is noticeable,' her fingers returned to her chin, 'and this one in my head.' She parted her hair and rubbed it. 'I'm lucky my hair is so thick. The rest are well hidden . . . Lee tells me that he doesn't notice them. Liar!' She smiled briefly. She was glad Lee *didn't* make an issue about the scars left by the assault. But she dismissed that thought and said angrily instead, 'Those bastards! I hope they rot in hell with everybody else like them.'

'I hope they do.' Esmine lowered her voice to a whisper, 'You should try not to blame every single person here for what they did though Sis. If you do, you will be falling into the same trap they're in. Stereotyping, generalising, failing to see any other part of us other than colour.' She had tried to use the gentlest of her voices.

Joy suddenly became impatient and cross. 'For God's sake Esmine, don't give me any of this, *I have a lot of friends who are white and there are good and bad in every kind*. People who use statements like that are just trying to excuse their racism. They really get under my skin. They are the same kind of people who say they never notice colour. Bloody liars! I don't know who they are trying to fool. They all notice colour. We are all just a *colour* to them.

'This country is packed with bigots. They are all conditioned that way. It is part of their upbringing, part of their culture. Some of them try to override it but the majority of them just wallow in it and would happily destroy us to prove it. So how am I supposed to know who is who? I can't go through life trying to vet every single person on the street!'

'Joy, you are making it all much worse than it really is. I'm not going to run away, because of a few fools. And it *is* a few, Joy. And even if it wasn't, I have my friends here, my life. Everything I know is here. So nobody is going to drive me out! Nobody!'

Joy felt so drained she couldn't answer. She only shook her head and sighed.

After a long silence she said to her sister, 'You know that you are very important to me don't you?'

Esmine squeezed their bodies together, 'Umm, I do.'

'It is really important to me to have your understanding.'

'I am trying Joy.' She hesitated then said, 'Joy will you be honest with me?'

'I'll try.'

'Are you really going back for yourself. Or do you want to do it for Daddy?'

Joy turned her words round in her mind. 'To be honest Essy, sometimes I don't even know. What I do know is that my heart is bleeding all the time because I know how important it would have been to *him* to go back.' She bit her lips. 'I know that he didn't want it just for himself but for us too. He didn't want us to live out our lives not knowing what it is truly like to be free.' She turned to look at Esmine but she showed no sign of wanting to interrupt her.

'You remember Daddy used to tell us about carrying sticks to burn coal?' Esmine nodded.

'I used to find it hard to imagine until we went home for the first time and saw them doing it in the country.' She turned to Esmine, 'Do you remember?'

'Yes.'

'When they made a mound with the sticks, they lit it from underneath and it burnt slowly and the sticks turned into coal.' Joy smiled to herself.

'Daddy said he used to carry sticks up hills and down gullies to burn coal, for trucks from town to collect. God they struggled! Carrying sticks and breaking stones!' She sighed.

'So you know what *I am* Esmine?' She looked at Esmine and waited. Esmine shook her head.

'Well I am that mound of sticks, that coal hill. All Daddy did was carry the sticks and set me in place. He knew that it would only be a matter of time before someone put a flame to me.' She shivered, 'Those creeps who kicked the hell out of me and countless others have been throwing flames on me for ages. And Sis, I'm burning!

'When I walk down the street minding my own business and somebody I have never set eyes on calls out, "*black bitch*", or "*nigger*", for me that is more fuel for the bonfire. So I keep burning. I burn every day Esmine. So unless I can find a way to stop the flames, I'm going to burn out.'

Esmine shook her head and sighed.

Joy continued, looking vacantly ahead, 'Just like those black people you see, walking down the street talking to themselves. Like the countless numbers you see in their mental hospitals. In their jails. Cleaning their streets. Or just cleaning. At the bottom of every ladder you'll find one of us. Holding it up. Waiting for the chance to step up, but knowing that we'll never get that chance . . . I tell you Mummy and Daddy are lucky . . .'

'Oh Joy. You don't believe *that*.'

'I do mean it baby sis. I do.'

'Joy you really frighten me sometimes.'

'I don't mean to, but I have come to realise that facing the truth can be very frightening.' She groaned, 'The truth frightens me.'

There seemed nothing more to say so Joy crawled into bed and watched her sister as she finished her fingers, painted her toe nails, plucked her eyebrows and applied vitamin E cream to her face and neck. Joy felt an old weight pressing down on her and was glad that back in London Janet would be there to provide distraction for both of them.

Fifteen

Janet packed the rest of her belongings ready for Esmine to collect. She stood by the bin bags and suitcase, her arms folded tightly into her body, sighing repeatedly and shifting from one leg to the other.

She still didn't feel in control. Sometimes she was fine, would go to bed, sleep and not dream. Now and again, she was able to hold down a temporary job, even go out socially with Esmine and old friends from college. The next moment, without warning, the dream would come and she would wake, terrified. She was still plagued by guilt, obsessed that she was being watched, that she was just living on borrowed time, waiting for the prophesied evil to strike her down.

She looked furtively around the flat. It would be a relief to leave the memory of that awful incident with her father behind. When there was no one else in the house, no television or radio on, nobody talking or laughing, she still felt him, saw him, strutting around, screaming at her, prophesying her damnation. Perhaps moving out would erase that awful fear of sinking, a millstone around her neck.

Janet moved around the bags and stood by the door rubbing her neck. She looked at her watch – a couple of hours before Esmine was due to arrive. She couldn't stay in the flat all that time. She had to go out.

She went to the park and sat by the pond, her teeth gnawing at the insides of her cheek, her eyes focused on the water.

She tried to recapture the feeling of warmth and security of those days in the bathroom with her mother. She couldn't! Of late she'd been finding it increasingly difficult. What was more, each day saw the feeling receding even further, to be replaced by a growing fear of water. Of drowning.

She stood up, not sure now why she had chosen to come. But it was either that or go back to the flat. She sat down again, shivering. A dog barking behind her distracted her for a moment. She looked round to see it scampering in front of its owner. At least there was company.

She turned back to the pond. The water was still, harmless. The ducks were on the other side. She got up and walked tentatively to the edge. *I won't allow him to make me afraid of everything.*

She stood looking into the pond, fighting her impulse to turn and run. The dog barked again behind her. She turned to see it charging towards her, its owner still some way in the distance.

She realized that he was running to jump in the pond. Forgetting her closeness to the edge, she took a step back, slipped and fell.

She felt the impact of the water, the violence of the sudden sharp coldness. She felt her face go under, was aware of a burning sensation in her nose and the back of her throat as the first flood of water forced its way into her mouth, stopping in her throat and blocking the passage of air. Panicking, she gulped, unable to swallow or cough. She tried desperately to stand up, to swim, to save herself, but, flailing helplessly, she couldn't work out which way was up. The dog jumped in.

Frantically she grasped at it, her hands connecting with the sodden fur. It struggled and yelped, fighting to free itself, its sharp teeth sinking into her hand. She yanked herself away, an overwhelming pain in her chest building up to her face, her throat, her whole body. She thought she would burst.

The owner of the dog sprinted up to the pond, tearing his coat off as he ran. Stepping down in the pond he grabbed Janet firmly around the waist and pulled her out. He dumped her, face down, on the grass, slapping her hard on the back.

They kept her overnight in the hospital.

Esmine picked her up and took the rest of the week off work to be with her.

A couple of nights later she lay awake in her room, back, it seemed, to where she had been months before: petrified of living, frightened to die. Like the rest of the house, her room was full of light. There were flowers and plants everywhere, prints and paintings. They stood out, making her feel more estranged from reality. Oh God, I'm in limbo. I'm no part of this world and I've turned my back on *Your* world. I have no home. What's going to happen to me? What else is going to happen to me? Why don't you just let it happen. Get it over and done with now.

She remained prostrate on the bed, listening, waiting for something to happen . . . anything.

Janet's eyes bolted open. Incredibly, she had slept, the whole night through. The light was coming in through the curtains. For a moment she didn't know where she was.

Her eyes met flowers in a fireplace, moved up to a ballerina on the wall. Like a stork, on tiptoe, the other leg hoisted, parallel with her arm that stretched above her head. A picture next to that, a woman, not unlike someone she knew, black, naked. Sitting, but tilted back, taut body, one breast just barely visible, cane rows forming a crown on her head.

She remembered. Joy. She was in Esmine's house. Janet glanced sideways at the clock: eleven. She rubbed her eyes. She might have been waking from a general anaesthetic. Hours of life obliterated. No dream. It had been neither blissful nor painful; just empty, a gap. She wondered whether that was what it felt like to be dead.

The house was so quiet. She sat up and listened. She wondered suddenly whether the rapture had come. Whether Jesus had come riding on clouds to gather the saints away. She strained her ears to catch any sign of life. There were cars but that didn't mean anything. *Two will be in the bed. One will be taken the other left.* That was how the Bible described the desolation following the rapture.

She got out of bed and opened the curtains, looked up to the sky. The clouds were still. There was no sign of the raptured saints riding on them with their lord.

Janet sighed, turned back into the room, wishing that her doom would come now and get it over and done with. She hated the waiting.

She moved away from the window. A print on the other side of the wall caught her eye. A woman scantily dressed, in white, contrasting with the darkness of her skin, embracing herself, eyes closed, lips quivering. She looked again. *Can't be! It was moving . . . the lips were moving!* She pressed her eyelids together and looked again. *Oh God, yes. It is moving . . .*

Janet swallowed and turned away but she had to look again. She squeezed her throat and swallowed, turning slowly to face the picture once more. She looked at it and blinked and looked again. No! It was smiling but not moving. *Thank God. It's not moving.*

Restless, she walked across the room and sat in front of the mirror by the large Victorian dressing table. Esmine had recently paid for her to have her hair plaited with extensions. The artistry on her head did not match the face below it.

Janet still could not come to terms with the way she looked. She peered deeply into her eyes. It was as if she was standing outside her own body watching herself. She made a scratching noise with her throat. The noise that she remembered old people at her church making when something made them sick, when they wanted to show scorn and disdain.

The bones in her face were hardly covered with flesh, her eyes were sunk deep into her head and were red with constant fear and weeping. Perhaps if her skin were not so pale she would not look so sickly.

An overwhelming sense of depression came over her, a sadness for the loss of her former self, a loss of the part of her that at least had some little choice and control.

She leaned back in the chair. Before her illness she had been so frightened of dying. She was never sure that she would have made it in to the Heavenly Home. Now, she felt death would be welcome. At least it would be *something* – an event, a reality. A way out of this dreadful uncertainty. And so many people would be free of me: my family, disgraced by my life, Esmine, dear Esmine . . . and Joy. Joy could have her sister back.

Janet sprang to her feet when she heard the knock on the door. 'Come in.'

Esmine came into the room, smiling. 'Hi. What's happened to everyone today? I thought you had all been struck down with some kind of sleeping sickness. I've just hammered down Joy's door – she's desperately late for work.'

Janet got up and received a peck on the cheek, sitting back on the side of the bed.

Esmine sat next to her. 'I'm so glad I don't have to work today. I'm wacked.' The corner of Janet's mouth went up in a half-smile. She wanted to thank her friend again but she stopped herself. At this rate she'd be thanking someone every minute.

Esmine looked at her with concern. 'Did you sleep well?'

'Not bad.'

'Managed without the tablets?'

'Just about.'

'Great.' She stood up, 'Do you want to be left alone for a while?'

'Oh no! I'm fine. I was just going to have a shower.'

'I'll fix myself something in the meantime. Come down when you're finished, okay?'

'Esmine?'

Esmine turned to face her, 'Yes?'

Janet stood up, feeling pathetic beside the upright figure of Esmine. She tried to raise herself to reach her but she could not muster the strength so she relaxed into her slouch.

'I just want to thank you again for having me . . . for looking after me . . . I know we are friends but if I ever become a burden please tell me . . .'

Esmine held her hand and smiled into her eyes. 'You are right . . . We are friends and friends can never be a burden.'

Sixteen

In the weeks that followed Joy had to fight off telling Janet to pull her wretched self together. She hated coming in after work to find her moping around, talking in Biblical riddles.

Joy tried to convince herself that she didn't mind Janet's irregular contributions to the bills, when she occasionally found temp work. That wasn't the issue. She couldn't stand people being defeatist, giving up and not fighting. She hated confusion and depression.

More than that she felt that Esmine was being put under pressure by Janet, making her anxious and worried all the time.

Joy got in her car and pulled away from her office, resolved to do something about it tonight. It was her yoga class evening at the gym. Janet would have to go to the beginner's class, start helping herself. Joy vowed to think of other things as well.

She sighed and accelerated across the lights as they changed to red, looking in her mirror to ensure no police car lurked behind her.

After the class Esmine met them as arranged in the club's bar. 'Was that all right Janet?' Esmine eyed her friend with concern. Janet nodded.

Joy tutted quietly and went to order more drinks, not wanting to hear if Janet said she hadn't enjoyed it. Whatever she feels, Joy thought, she will have to go again next week.

She returned and sat down smiling, disguising her thoughts.

'Janet says she's glad you persuaded her to come out,' Esmine said, hopelessly fanning the cigarette smoke that formed a cloud in the bar.

'Oh?' Joy looked questioningly at Janet.

Janet fingered her glass of pineapple juice. 'Yes, it wasn't as hard as I thought it would be.'

'So next week again,' Joy said emphatically; 'and you can join me at least once a week at home.' She looked briefly around the tracksuited bar, 'There's nothing like exercises for calming the mind.'

Janet nodded, taking a small sip of her drink.

Esmine drained her glass. 'Can you two hurry up?' She fanned in front of her face again. 'This smoke is killing me.'

Joy finished her drink, watching Janet push hers away. 'Don't you want the rest Janet?'

'No thanks,' she whispered apologetically.

Esmine stood up, her hand on her friend's arm 'Don't worry. Let's go.'

The following day, Joy gave Janet a day off from exercising but asked her to join in the day after that. Joy hated having to interrupt her own routine to explain. She hated being patient, but felt it would be worth it.

So, at first it was one day a week then two. After the first month it was three. Joy insisted that it could never be less, 'You lose the benefit if you stop or if you are not consistent.'

One Saturday morning Esmine sat watching them, three shades of nail polish lined up on the coffee-table next to her, the emery board obedient under the guidance of her long thin fingers. She opened her mouth, remembered her promise, closed it without speaking. She told herself, instead, that Janet *was* getting the hang of it.

After they had done the usual routine they took the corpse

position and held it for two minutes of deep breathing. Joy was the first to open her eyes, raise her back off the floor, pull up her knees and stand up.

'I really don't know how you do that without your hands.' Esmine shifted her eyes from one nail polish to the next.

'You couldn't wait could you?'

'Wait for what?' Esmine smiled at Janet.

'To speak.'

'I can speak now can't I?' She continued to run the emery board across the tips of her nails.

Janet sat up too, pulling herself across the floor until her back rested on the settee.

'You did really well today Janet, really well. Can you feel it becoming easier?'

'Yes. I can stretch a little further each time.'

'I thought so too,' Esmine said.

'Esmine! I am going to tell you this last time. If you are going to watch us, you must not keep commenting in the middle . . .'

'Sorry. I just thought Janet was getting so far down with the back stretch.' She put down the emery board and surveyed the bottles of polish, 'Ummm, plum I think this week.'

Joy sat back on the floor as Janet went to shower.

Joy looked after her, still wondering whether she was doing the right thing, forcing her to exercise. She was so thin. At least she was eating something these days. And, Joy mused, she's not such a weakling as I first thought. She's fighting. She's trying. She works when she gets something to do and she never says no when I invite her out. Perhaps I've been hard on her.

Joy ensured that Janet was fully inside the bathroom before speaking, 'Esmine I've asked a therapist friend of mine to see Janet.'

'What? What did Janet say about it?'

'I haven't told her yet.'

'Joy, that's out of order.'

'Why?' Joy looked at her sister with challenge, 'She needs the help. She can't just go on like this.'

'I know, but you should have asked her first.'

'And have her say no . . .'

'As if Janet is confident enough to say *no* to you.'

'I'm just trying to help her, Esmine.'

'What if . . .'

'What if nothing. She needs to talk to somebody.'

Esmine sighed heavily.

'She does. Even you have to admit that whatever I've suggested so far, like yoga and socialising, have helped.'

'I suppose so, but I don't know . . . a therapist . . .'

'Well I've made the appointment and paid for some . . . the session. It's next week.'

Esmine shook her head. 'I just don't believe you sometimes.'

Joy ran her hands over her folded legs, 'Whatever happens it won't do her any harm.' She stopped and thought, 'And anyway if she's going to stay here when I leave . . .' She watched Esmine's face growing more pensive. '. . . I don't want her being a liability to you.'

'She'll never be that.'

Joy pursed her lips, '. . . Especially since you're vowed to celibacy . . .'

'I never said that!'

'Well your actions suggest it.'

Esmine sucked her teeth, 'Joy I'm really hungry.'

Joy got up. 'Okay let's go and do the breakfast.'

Seventeen

Joy knocked firmly on the door, conscious of Janet's nervousness. She had made the appointment for eleven. It was her day to have lunch with Esmine, so she could go straight to the restaurant afterwards.

She turned to Janet, 'My friend has her consulting room in her attic.'

Janet nodded, her teeth firmly clenched.

Janet avoided Joy's eyes. She didn't know why she was allowing herself to be so totally manipulated by Joy. She sighed. *Perhaps because I have to show gratitude. She didn't have to agree to have me in her home.*

The door opened. A small, softly spoken woman greeted them, extending her hand to Janet, 'I'm Anita. Do come in.'

Janet stepped into the hall, moving aside for Joy and Anita to exchange kisses.

'We'll go upstairs Janet,' Anita said, smiling. 'Joy, you know where everything is. Make yourself whatever you want.'

'Thanks. I've actually got some work to do so I'll just get on with it.' She touched Janet's arm, 'See you later.'

Janet nodded.

'Do sit down Janet.' Anita motioned to one of the two armchairs

139

placed opposite each other. 'Would you like something to drink?'

'No thanks, I'm fine.'

Anita sat down on the other chair.

Janet relaxed a little.

Anita didn't have the notebook or tape recorder she had imagined. The room was almost like a sitting room, a sofa in one corner, two arm chairs, a large oak desk. Plants, books and fresh flowers on shelves. Black and white prints, African and Caribbean wood carvings on the walls.

'Janet we'll have a talk for about forty-five minutes but we can of course go on longer if you wish. Okay?' Her voice was as Janet had expected, soft and enquiring.

Janet swallowed and nodded, not quite able yet to hold Anita's eyes which were looking into hers. She could only focus from her braided hair down to her forehead.

'In this session Janet I would like you to start where you feel able to . . .'

'This session? I didn't know there would be more.'

'Yes. If you want them . . . Joy paid for ten sessions but it is up to you to decide if you need them. She can be reimbursed.'

Janet nodded and sighed heavily.

'Okay?' Anita sat with her fingers lightly resting on her legs.

Janet cleared her throat and nodded. 'I'm not sure where to start. What has Joy told you?'

'Nothing.'

'I see.' Locking her fingers, she met Anita's eyes. 'I feel . . . I feel that something awful is going to happen to me . . .' She stopped, expecting Anita to interject.

Anita gazed steadily at her.

'. . . I'm convinced that my father has the spirit of discerning, is able to get straight to God and ask him to hurt me, has asked God to punish me, to punish me . . .' Janet stopped and swallowed. She was hearing her words as if they were coming from someone else. She'd never heard herself say any of it like that before. Her fingers relaxed and she heard herself telling everything about her childhood. Of how terrified she had always been. How trapped and frightened she was and how desperate she was for release.

Joy's eyes widened when she saw Janet's puffy red eyes. Resting her hand gently on her arm, she thanked Anita.

'Goodbye Janet. See you same time next week.'

Janet nodded and allowed herself to be directed to the car.

She told Joy that she preferred to go straight home, so Joy drove her back before meeting Esmine in a new Caribbean restaurant near Anita's home. Joy found it too small and cramped for her liking but she loved the food. Since she had discovered it a few months before, she often went a long way out of her way to sample yet another of the dishes.

'So how did it go?' Esmine asked, tucking into her fried dumplings, ackee and salt fish.'

'I don't know, she had obviously been crying.'

'Joy, I hope you did the right thing you know.'

'Well, she said in the car she'd finish the sessions . . .'

'What sessions?'

'I had booked ten sessions for her.' Joy avoided her sister's eyes.

'You didn't tell me that . . .'

'Oh Esmine, it's done now. Let's just leave it.'

Esmine stared at Joy.

'This is good!' Joy said, ignoring her, 'You should have the callaloo. It's brilliant!'

Esmine let go of her irritation reluctantly. 'This is good too.'

Joy put down her cutlery. 'Did I tell you that Lee and I had a bit of an argument yesterday?'

'What's new? You are always provoking him.'

Joy sipped her carrot juice, determined to get it off her chest

141

despite her sister. '*He* accused me of being jealous of *that* woman. Can you believe it? Who could be jealous of that ignoramus?'

'You! You are always going on about her.'

'I'm not!'

'Joy, do keep your voice down.'

'Why? This place is so noisy, no one could hear us.' She looked round. The take-away queue was building up, all the tables were taken and there was a queue for them too.

Esmine smiled suddenly. 'You amuse me you know Joy. Why are you putting pressure on him and insisting on fidelity when you're leaving him?'

'That's not the point! He knows the score. Anyway I'm faithful to *him*.'

'Joy! God! Your nose is going to touch the wall over there.' Esmine looked behind her, open mouthed.

'I have been for ages . . . and anyway I'm always discreet.'

Esmine raised her eyebrows and continued eating.

'Not long now eh?'

'Oh.' The question took Joy off guard.

Esmine had not mentioned her going back for ages, and she'd been careful to avoid the topic until she felt her sister was ready.

'So what are you looking forward to most then?' Esmine's gaze fixed on her. It was seconds before Joy answered. When she did she was sure Esmine was sorry she had asked.

'I'm looking forward to a lot. I dream of it. Finally going to the airport with you and all of my friends. I want to have a big dinner party before I leave, curry goat and the like. The weekend before I go . . . so I can spend the last weekend with you.' She reached out and took her sister's hand. 'I don't want you to cry . . . I want us to do all our crying before we get to the airport. I want us to get the crying over now.'

'You want us to cry for nine months?' Esmine withdrew her hand, serious.

'If you want to, and if it's going to stop you crying at the airport. Anyway, it should be a celebration ... We'll get to the airport, car loads of us. We'll talk about food on the way, roast breadfruit ackee and saltfish, paw-paw juice ... That's what I want my first meal to be. When we get to the airport there'll be a lot of cuddling and holding, but no crying. Do you hear?'

Esmine shrugged.

Joy smiled, trying to make her voice light-hearted. 'Do you remember Mummy used to tell us that when they left Jamaica for England, people went to the airport with white handkerchiefs and waved to them as they climbed the steps to the plane?'

'You don't want us to do that, do you?' Esmine asked half-joking.

'Do you want to?' Joy asked.

'Of course not!'

'Anyway, just as we're sharing a joke, I'll go. With everyone laughing. I'd have made you promise before to come and see me at Christmas. In fact I'll see that you buy your ticket before I leave ...'

'How about Lee? Are you going to make him promise too?'

'I'll leave it up to him. But I hope he won't want to.'

'Poor man.'

Joy shook her head, not prepared to talk about that again. 'Shall we get our bill? We have to be getting back.'

Esmine looked at her watch. 'Okay.'

Joy took it. 'It's my turn to pay this week.'

'It's always your turn when it's cheap.'

Joy half-smiled.

'Go on ... You haven't got there yet. You're still at passport control.'

'You want to hear more?' Joy wrote out the cheque.

'I suppose I might as well.'

'Well, since there will be no white handkerchiefs flying for me

143

I'll just make my way into the aircraft . . . I pity the person who'll be unfortunate enough to sit next to me because I'll talk non-stop about nothing in particular. Just to make the time go quicker. Then I'll try and get permission to go to the cockpit just to remind myself of the first time I went home . . . when I get there I'll feel, Oh God, that blessed day . . .'

'One of Daddy's gems,' Esmine muttered.

But Joy's eyes were shining. 'The heat will be like a hot blanket thrown over me as I step off the aircaraft, but I won't care. I'll have had my hair plaited and have dragged my shorts on just before landing. I'll feel like kissing the tarmac . . . but I suppose I had better not do that. But I *know* I'll smell the earth . . .'

'You'll what?' Esmine furrowed her brow. 'On second thoughts, don't tell me. It'll be too profound for me.'

'Then I'll begin to thaw out, the accumulated toxins in my body will slowly begin to seep out. I'll try to wait patiently at Norman Manley airport as they look sceptically at my passport. I'll frown, just like the guy who is checking my passport. When he asks, *a you dis*? I'll simply say, "Yes, I was younger then". And he'll make some joke or other, and whether it's funny or not I'll laugh. I'll watch as they turn my case inside out. Or if I'm really lucky, I'll just collect it and walk straight out to one of the porters who'll take me to my friends.

'Eventually I'll get the job I want. I won't be too fussy at first but eventually I'll get exactly what I want . . . Before my car arrives I'll go everywhere by minibus and have my life squeezed out of me . . .'

Esmine made a face and got up, 'Like that time on the way to Hope Gardens.'

Joy smiled broadly, 'Oh yes! Just like that time . . .'

Eighteen

Joy and Esmine went together to collect a parcel from their father's old workmate, Lenny. He had just returned from a holiday to Jamaica and had brought things back for them.

For some reason people of her parents' generation always reminded Joy of one another. Perhaps it was the matter of fact way they spoke – their accents, a slight mixture of South London, the rest still stubbornly Jamaican; or the calculated dryness of their humour, their natural protectiveness towards the younger generation; or just their ready hospitality.

Joy watched with mounting eagerness as Mr Walker shared out mangoes – precious, because they were now out of season in Jamaica – patties, ground provisions like sweet potatoes, yam, dasheen, and the bush tea – mint and fever grass, Joy's favourite. She had only recently realised that it was very much like the lemon verbena tea she bought in health shops in London.

Mrs Walker insisted that they stay for dinner, saying she welcomed the company. Their own children were grown up and had dinner with them only on Sundays. They had steamed fish and ground provisions fresh from back home.

Joy felt looked after. She didn't even mind Mr Walker bringing up the subject of their father's death, saying he missed his best mate, or his question about how often they went to the cemetery, or them discussing her impending trip, or listening to how *tough* it was in Jamaica.

'You really need to have money and a good job to make it out there,' Lenny said gloomily. He went on to tell them how he had met a lot of people who had left England to return who were now in dire straits. 'Many of them are thinking of coming back! They have no choice. They just struggling and struggling, with no sign of things getting better. The money they take out with them just finish off.'

'So you must really think about it before you go back and throw you future away,' his wife Daisy concluded, sombrely.

Joy felt her sister's eyes on her and was glad when the conversation eventually shifted.

On their way home, they passed their old home. Joy was tempted to stop for a minute, but she suddenly remembered the hearse by the gate and she sped on by.

Her mind turned to her father's story of her birth. They had had no garden and so no earth, so her father had no space in which to plant her navel string. He had kept it in a box for nearly two years. Then he went home to Jamaica on holiday.

The day after he got there he went to his father's old ground. He picked a black mango from one of the trees, sat under the tree and ate the mango. After he had finished, he took the seed and planted it with Joy's navel string.

When Esmine was born, they had a house with a garden, so he planted her navel string under a shrub in the garden in London.

After their parents had died, in all their confusion and pain and their hurry to get out of the house, Esmine and Joy had forgotten to take a cutting of the shrub before they left.

'That's why you have to go and I am staying,' Esmine had said. And perhaps she had been right.

They stopped at a wine bar not far from their home. They sipped cocktails without speaking until Joy said how much she hated winter. 'The days are too short.'

'You'll be away from it soon . . .'

Joy smiled, 'Not soon enough.' She pressed her fingers into her forehead, trying to uncrease the frown etched there.

Esmine watched her for a moment. 'Tired?'

'Yes. I was in court today trying to get this wretched man to increase child maintenance payments to his daughter. He's only giving his ex-wife a miserly ten pounds a week. God knows how a child can be supported on that . . .'

'Was it increased?'

'Of course. But it always takes me ages to unwind after unnecessary appearances like that.' Joy sipped her drink, feeling suddenly lonely despite the packed bar and the jollity of its patrons. 'God knows how you get through life without someone to help you get rid of the tension.'

Esmine smirked. 'That's not the only way to get rid of tension. Anyway I thought you said your exercises did that for you.'

'Well they do, but not as fully.' Joy pressed her temples.

'So Lee is coming round tonight then?' Esmine asked cynically.

'Yes,' Joy said, oblivious of the subtle criticism. 'I called him from work. He's coming late because he took some work home, so I'll have a couple of hours sleep before he arrives.'

'So the poor bloke will be the only one who goes into work tomorrow without sleep.' Esmine shook her head.

'He'll have a song on his lips though.'

'A bet that's not all he'll have on them.'

'You dirty girl.' Joy pushed her gently on the arm.

Esmine sighed, looking around absent-mindedly at the trendy young set in the bar.

'What's wrong?' Joy rubbed her gently on her arm.

Esmine scowled.

'What is it?'

147

'Did you hear what Lenny said?'

Joy had known it was going to be only a matter of time before Esmine brought this up, but she played ignorant anyway.

'About what?'

Esmine did not disguise her exasperation, 'You know what I mean . . . about how difficult it is in Jamaica. Don't bury your head in the sand Joy. It won't be easy. People are running back here every day.'

'I know . . .' Joy said simply, not really prepared to defend her decision again.

'Joy, you have to face facts.'

Joy shifted warily in her seat, wishing she was drinking alone among the strangers around her.

Esmine continued pressing home her point, 'If I were you I'd be careful that you don't end up like one of the thousands who have to eat their words.'

'Don't exaggerate,' Joy said finally, ready to leave. 'For everyone who comes back I'm sure there are four or five who stay and don't have a moment's regret.'

'Yes but the ones who do, they are the ones who make the news. They are pitiful. They struggled here for donkey's years.'

'As Daddy used to say . . .'

'Then they come back in a worse position than when they first arrived. Some of them can't even come back because they'd thought after sweating blood . . .'

Joy looked at her sister, wondering if there was any particular purpose to her using their father's sayings so frequently.

'. . . They would not need to beg to come back. They hadn't even bothered to get the prized British passport, so all some of them can get is six months.'

'A prison sentence,' Joy said drily.

Esmine ignored her. 'All that labouring and sacrificing and all they can get is six months.'

'Serves them right, I have no sympathy. I would prefer to clean the toilets back home than stay here!'

'You would *not*.'

'I would. If that was all there was . . .'

'You should hear yourself. You can't even tell the truth.' Esmine got up. 'Let's go.'

Joy followed her, seething. Back in the car she unleashed, 'You always spoil my evenings.'

'What?' Esmine shouted. 'You just can't face the truth. Well it's up to you. If you want to go blindly and spoil your life, as everyone keeps warning you, don't come crawling back and ask for my support.'

'Listen Esmine,' Joy said as she drove off, too fast, 'this subject is closed! I do not want to discuss it with you again! All you think about is your bloody self. You don't really care what the hell happens to me, so don't pretend that all this concern is about *me*.'

Esmine waited for her to calm down before she spoke again. They were a couple of turnings from the house. 'This *is* your home Joy.'

'Esmine, I said I don't want . . .'

'Well why don't you jump out of the car then? Because I'm going to have my say. I'm not Lee.'

'Don't you dare . . .'

'Just be quiet! You can't always have your own way.' Esmine dug her heels in, 'You always chose not to remember what Mummy used to tell us.'

Joy was shaking with anger. It crossed her mind to stop the car, take the keys and leave Esmine sitting there.

'We struggled to get an identity for ourselves here Joy. You know as well as I do that Mummy and Daddy, Mummy *especially*, taught us to refute the distorted image that the whites created for us. We were taught to define ourselves, to be sure of who we were and where we were coming from, Africa or Jamaica or wherever, but to claim this country as our own too. Don't tell me you've forgotten how confident we were about what we wanted to accept or reject. How we even refused to play with dolls because there were either white ones or black ones that were not like us but caricatures . . . the way we thought they wanted to see us.'

Joy exhaled loudly.

'We loved ourselves, our heritage, but we *still* felt we could be called British. We felt it wasn't selling out or compromising as some people back then said.'

Esmine's voice became suddenly quiet, 'We have a lot to thank our mother for Joy. She taught us all that.' Esmine stopped and looked at her sister's profile.

Joy said nothing. It was as if she was still being lectured by her mother back in the days when she was not allowed to answer back.

'Did you hear what I've been saying Joy?'

'I am not deaf,' Joy snapped.

Esmine glared at her. 'So long as you heard me.' She sat back, folded her arms and turned the radio up loud.

And suddenly Joy felt an overwhelming resentment of her mother, quickly replaced by a powerful guilt. She bit her lips. Her mother, she thought suddenly, *had* struggled for them, *had* taught them a lot. She owed her so much, there was so much to be grateful to her for.

So taken up had she been with her father's lost dreams that she had not allowed herself, up to now, to see that he might not have been right in every way.

Joy could not admit it to her sister then, or agree that it meant *she* had to stay in England, but she began to understand and respect Esmine's position. Esmine had as much right to stay in England and fight as *she* had to return to Jamaica.

Nineteen

It was Joy's idea to make the trip to the Midlands to see Janet's family. Janet's therapy sessions seemed to be doing some good. She was eating again and was less fatalistic.

The trip, Joy hoped, would speed things up, get her to make some decision, either to go back home or to stay. Joy needed to know for Esmine's sake. She couldn't leave Esmine with the burden of Janet.

Janet had reacted with terror. She *couldn't*, she protested. She couldn't bear the thought of being in the same room with her father, of dealing with her mother's sorrow. She was certain it wouldn't do any good and would set back the progress she had made with Anita. But Joy was adamant. It was the only way to confirm her better health, she argued, to make sure she was now on firmer ground. And she ought to do that for Esmine's sake. She couldn't be dependent for ever. Janet was shocked into silence. Still terrified, she allowed herself, for Esmine, to be argued down.

Only when Joy announced that they were nearly there did she speak detached and wary, 'When I phoned yesterday to confirm that we were coming Mum cried . . . I hope she's not expecting too much.'

Joy raised an eyebrow. 'I hope it will be all right.' She felt easier, more patient with Janet now than she had felt at first.

Esmine turned a sympathetic look on Janet, 'I'm as nervous as hell.'

When they arrived at the church it was five minutes to eleven. The doors were still locked.

'You sure we've got the right church?' Joy asked, looking across at the door.

'Of course. Janet has been coming here . . .' Esmine said with impatience.

'Nearly all my life.'

'So where is everybody?' Joy asked.

'It's not eleven yet.'

'It's two minutes to go. Do they arrive on the dot then?'

'You joking.'

There was no mistaking it, Joy thought, Janet's voice is shaking. She felt a slight wave of guilt but dismissed it.

'Everyone waits for everyone else to get here first and the one who arrives first huffs and puffs about those who arrive after.'

'It'll be worth waiting for, I'm sure,' Esmine lied.

'Do you mind turning the tape off now please Joy?'

Joy turned round to look at Janet, 'Why? It's not too loud is it?'

'No,' Esmine whispered, 'We don't want to offend the brethren when they come. Reggae's not exactly appropriate Sunday music outside a Pentecostal church is it?'

'Oh sorry. I forgot,' Joy said, removing the tape.

Janet sighed heavily as she watched her parents' car pull up. She hadn't seen them for nearly two years. Not since that day back in college when they had found her with Roger.

'They're here,' she said feebly.

Esmine turned and rested her hand on her lap. 'You all right?' Janet nodded.

Esmine got out of the car and opened the door for her. As soon as she got out her mother looked across and saw her.

'God be praised,' she shouted.

Janet was rooted to the spot until Esmine threaded their hands together and walked her across the road.

Joy locked up and followed them.

Esmine stood, not quite sure what to do with her hands as Janet was swept up by her mother. For a moment she was not sure whether Janet had fainted. Her whole body was limp.

Her mother's eyes were closed. 'She has come home! Glory! I told Sam that you would come back to the Lord. The Lord works in mysterious ways His wonders to perform.' She released her daughter, then grabbed her again.

Janet pulled away, smoothed her clothes back in place, looked up and was face to face with her father. Neither of them moved or spoke. Finally, he stretched out his hand to her.

Janet's hands came up slowly from her side, barely meeting his before withdrawing.

Mrs Murray turned and shook Joy and Esmine by the hand.

The pastor did the same. He did not smile.

'God bless you both.'

Mrs Murray raised her hand to heaven again, 'God be praised. Let us go and open up. My heart is overflowing with joy.'

Joy looked at Esmine and Janet and led them, behind the pastor and his wife, into the church.

Everybody seemed to arrive at once. One moment strained silence reverberated in the church, the next, it was almost full. Nothing of its Anglican past remained. There were no icons, no pictures of the Apostles, the Blessed Virgin, no crucifixion scenes.

What decorated the church were posters with scripture verses and flower surrounds. There were two on the rostrum, one spelling out in bold black the first commandment. The other read: *Come out from among them and be he separate.*

Joy looked around the church as she heard the contained shuffles of yet another group arriving.

The brethren might have been dressed by a special top designer – the women's co-ordinated dresses, hats, shoes and bags. The men were all suited, hats left on a rack by the front door, ties, if not totally in vogue, worn as if lately off some top shop in town, shoes polished to perfection, cuff-links and tie pins shining. The children were like miniature adults in the Victorian mould, tightly contained in crisp Sunday best.

Everyone came in quietly, almost on tiptoe, greeting those within reach with a smile or a kiss; if out of reach, with a slight nod. Only the women kissed. Each then knelt, closed eyes and whispered prayers before rising.

One woman in particular caught Joy's eye. She wore shocking pink taffeta with a large bow at the side. She took a seat in the row just in front of them. She did not kneel like the others but stood, covered her mouth with her palm, closed her eyes and whispered her prayer. She looked around with a smile when she had finished, smoothed her taffeta under her bottom and sat down.

Joy smiled, looking at Esmine to see if she had noticed.

Esmine was serious. Looking fixedly ahead.

Janet was looking at her lap.

The three women were in the middle row, half-way down the pews, Janet sandwiched between the sisters. This did not deter those who saw her. Kisses were blown in her direction. Those who could, kissed her loudly on her mouth and turned with curious smiles to her companions.

The pastor was joined on the rostrum by several other men, deacons, evangelists and elders of the church. Finally, two female evangelists took their places beside them.

Without warning, the empty seats on their right were taken by the choir. They marched out from the vestry in purple gowns and white hats, smiling sweetly at the congregation. They too whispered their prayers. Six young girls with tambourines from the front row then moved out and stood directly in front of the congregation. Boys, last out of the vestry, tuned the drum, guitars and saxaphone.

One of the young women spoke, greeting the brethren and

directing them in the singing of choruses. As one chorus ended, so another began. The band played. The brethren clapped their hands and danced in the aisles.

Joy swayed, occasionally casting her eyes on the chorus sheet.

Janet did not move. She sang inaudibly, like a stifled ventriloquist, her eyes fastened on the wall in front of her.

At first Joy was anxious to make sure that her own movements were righteous. She had looked around self-consciously. But she realised that she couldn't distinguish her movements from that of the brethren. They rocked, swayed, jumped. So she relaxed and moved. She took further encouragement from the song leader, 'Come on brethren make use of the music . . . move to the glory of God . . . rock in the spirit . . .'

The sister in shocking pink taffeta did just that. Her hips went in one direction and the top half of her in another. She kept the same movement for each chorus. She smiled, clapped, looked around, threw her arms in the air, rocked and swayed.

Joy took a step forward so she could catch Esmine's eyes, savour the moment with her. Esmine's eyes were fixed on the chorus sheet. Joy was totally exhausted when the song leaders marched back into the choir.

Another sister replaced the song leaders. She was to lead the devotional.

'Before we sing our hymn, brethren, I want us all to stand and give three praises to the Lord . . . You know brethren . . .' She started to cry, 'As I walked in this morning and saw sister Janet, my heart . . .' She stopped and wiped her eyes, '. . . my heart became full, and I knew that the Lord had been speaking to me all this week.' She sniffed loudly.

The congregation groaned.

'You see brethren, all this week the song "Home once more, the prodigal returns to his home once more" has been going through my mind. Oh Glory to His name . . . So when I walked in and saw her, brethren, I knew that the Lord had been speaking to me.'

Joy felt the heat rise within her quickly moving up her neck, her ears and face, as the whole congregation joined with the sister in praises and weeping. She felt for Janet, who was rigid, oblivious of Esmine's hand that was resting on hers.

When it was quiet again the sister asked the brethren to stand and give Janet a hand. So they clapped. The music played and the lady in shocking pink taffeta danced in her seat. Joy and Esmine were given a special welcome and informed that God had brought them to the church for a special reason.

When the pastor stood up to deliver the message Joy felt she understood at last what the term sanctimonious meant. In the tense atmosphere outside the church she had not really looked at him properly. Now she had no choice.

He was not a tall man but he seemed to tower through and above the church.

Joy could see where Janet got her pale complexion and grey eyes, but that was where the resemblance ended.

Joy fixed her eyes on him because it was impossible to do otherwise. But as he spoke she found herself wondering whether, like her father, he had carried load back home, broken stone, worried about whether the corn he planted would grow. Or the rain would fall.

No, he wouldn't have struggled so much, she decided. With his pale complexion he would have had a better life than her father. He would have got into high school, got a good job when he left. He would have been proud of his fair skin. But he should be rejecting what his paleness stands for. All it proved was that a foremother had been raped by a slave-owner. How *could* he feel pride in her degradation and shame? They should *remember*, Joy thought – be angry and militant. But instead they boast. How *backward* they are, she thought.

Twenty

The pastor had started his message in his usual quiet, pleading way. Janet could have recited it with him. But she wasn't fooled. She found herself looking him up and down with growing anger. Looking past his black suit and tie, past his glittering tie pin and cuff-links. Past his shining white false teeth and righteous face – to him prancing in her room, frothing at the mouth.

Janet only focused on what he was saying when she heard him mention her name. She sighed and closed her eyes for a moment, bracing herself.

'I would like to glorify the Lord with the rest of the brethren this morning for bringing Sis Janet back to us today,' he had said evenly, looking in his daughter's general direction. 'I prayed. So I was confident that this day had to come. That is why brethren you know we must believe the Holy scriptures.'

Janet thought he sounded bored. Detached. But she knew that wouldn't last. He always started like that. He took time to warm up.

'. . . What do the scriptures say? *They that wait upon the Lord shall renew their strength, they shall mount up with wings like eagles, they shall walk and not be weary, they shall run and not faint.* Glory to His name.'

The pastor stopped and shook his head. 'It may not be the way we want it done. It may not happen when we want it, but as sure as night follows day, what He has promised He will do. Are you happy to see Sister Janet back, brethren? Let us stand then and give the Holy Ghost a hand.'

Janet bit her lips and shifted herself towards Esmine, 'God knows how much of this I can stand.'

Esmine rested her hand on her lap, 'You are doing marvellously. Hang on in there.'

That done, the pastor asked for another prayer.

An elderly man stepped forward from his seat behind the pastor. His prayer was long and intense, Janet being the main subject of it. He told God that she could have been numbered with the dead but his gracious mercy had spared her.

'. . . The cunning adversary took her out from among us but you searched for her, *and up through the mountain thunder riven and down to the valley deep, there arose a cry, rejoice for I have found my sheep . . .'*

Janet fought to keep her eyes closed.

Pastor Murray rose from his knees and opened his Bible. 'As you can see, the topic for today is, *Come out from among them and be ye separate says the Lord.*' He pointed without turning to the poster behind them. 'I believe the Lord wants to speak to us today, so do not hinder the spirit. Open your hearts and pray for me.'

Janet remembered her childhood fear of the intensity of her father's messages. Then, it had seemed to her that he knew the Bible from cover to cover.

He had done then as he was doing now. He asked the congregation to take up their Bibles. It could be 1 Corinthians, Ezra, Leviticus, Deuteronomy, Revelations, Genesis, backwards and forwards he went.

The congregation would find the scripture. Someone would stand and read. He would repeat the reading, translate into Jamaican, interpret, relate to their situation and then he would go to the next one and the next.

There were times when he would close his huge Bible and march around the rostrum, emphasise a point by thumping the pulpit or a well-positioned table. He would skip and shout, sing his words, beg them to listen to him, to praise the Lord with him, to clap hands with him.

When he was really moved in the spirit he would leap from the rostrum and skip like a billy goat down the aisle, daring anyone who had sinned that week and had not repented, not washed their garments in the blood of the lamb, to catch his eye. The spirit would lead him straight over to that unfortunate individual. He would hold that person's eyes as he talked to him, and the sinner would be hot and bothered but would not be able to move in his seat, not until the spirit had released him, until he knew what had to be done to make it right again with God.

Janet feared those times. She would pray then as she had never prayed before that he would not pick her out, that nothing would be revealed to him of what she may have done – those sins of omission or commission. She was sure she would not have been able to bear the chastisement of the Lord.

Now Pastor Murray scanned the congregation, resting his eyes over Janet's head. '. . . Many of you sitting there are frightened of hell fire, and so you should be . . .' He looked up to the ceiling, '. . . I am opening my mouth, Lord, I know you will fill it with words . . . For there, in the bottomless pit, the worms die not, and thirst is never quenched . . . For there will be weeping and wailing and gnashing of teeth.'

Janet was looking down at the Bible in her lap but she could feel his eyes on her.

'. . . Yes, you are frightened of all this but you love the pleasures of the world.' His voice was like crashing waves, smashing and recoiling against rock. Smash. Recoil.

'. . . Yes you have not come out from among them. You are not separated from them. You are still tied up and wrapped up and tangled up with them. Oh Jesus. But you can't fool the Lord! You

159

can't fool Him. His all-seeing eyes are watching you, tracking you down, following you wherever you go . . .'

The congregation groaned.

He stopped, as if giving his words time to sink in. The groaning stopped too. They watched, waiting for his words.

Janet raised her eyes slowly from her opened Bible.

His eyes were not exactly fixed on the three of them but his gaze hovered just above their row. She pressed her hands between her legs.

He moved away from the table, lowering his voice '. . . You know, brethren, we do suffer because of our sins. Don't let anyone fool you. We do.' He raised his voice then and made a fist with both hands. '. . . It may be sickness,' he stopped again and waited; 'it may even be death . . . Oh Jesus have mercy on me today . . .' He paced about the rostrum.

'. . . I do have to tell the truth, brethren, no matter how much it hurts. His words are in me like burning fire shut up in my bones and I cannot stay. I have a responsibility as you pastor and overseer. I have opened my mouth and the Lord has filled it with words.'

He stepped off the rostrum.

Janet's heart stopped.

He did not speak as he walked past the first row. Past the next and the next. He stopped by their row.

'. . . Yes, you will suffer as a result of your secret sins but He is still waiting to forgive. All you have to do is repent. Admit that you have fallen and come to him. Today! Today! Today!'

He sang the words. He pretended to be looking at nobody in particular but everyone could see that his eyes were fastened on his daughter.

'. . . Don't leave it for tomorrow because tomorrow may be too late. Come to Him and He will heal you of your sicknesses and your diseases. Don't think that you can sort things out yourself. You can't. Only the Almighty can make you right again. Only He can

160

throw out the seven devils that had taken a hold of you . . .'

He was crying as he spoke.

Groaning and crying broke out over the whole congregation.

He held on to the seat at the end of the row for support. He rocked to and fro as he sobbed. '. . . He can heal you . . . Oh anoint me Father . . . He can heal you . . .' Finally, exhausted, he fell to his knees, shaking, weeping and groaning.

Janet bit into her lips and looked down at her hands She would have liked to have got up and run out of the church, to have kept running and running until she fell down dead. *Why is he doing this to me? In front of my friends? Why did I follow Joy? What am I doing here?*

It seemed an eternity before the weeping and wailing ceased. He opened his eyes, motioned to the choir, closed them again, continuing to kneel as they stood and sang, 'Coming home, Coming home, Oh Lord I am coming home . . .'

Some of the brethren bowed their heads, others knelt, but they all wept together until the fabric of the building shook.

The pastor got up, walked back to the rostrum and waited a few moments before speaking again. 'If anyone feels the need for the saviour in their lives I would like you to come to the altar. You have heard the message. It was not from me but from the Lord.' He motioned to the choir again.

They sang, '*This World is not my home I'm only passing through. My treasures are laid up . . .*'

The pastor patted the air and the choir lowered their voices to a haunting whisper.

He spoke over their singing. '. . . He's pleading with you. You don't have to suffer any longer. You don't have to bear the shame and humiliation any longer. You don't have to be homeless . . . Come to Him. He'll provide rest for your restless soul . . .' No one moved.

He cut the air, his palm facing the choir. They stopped in mid sentence.

'Let us all be silent for a while. Let us listen for a moment. I would like everyone to stand. Everyone in the congregation who has feet. Everybody in the building please stand . . . Praise Him.'

He waited until they were all standing. His eyes scanned the congregation. 'Now. If you are saved . . . If you know Jesus as your personal saviour, I would like you to sit down. If you don't know him, please continue to stand . . . You cannot lie to Jesus.'

The brethren looked with self-satisfied grins at each other and sat down. Only Janet, her friends, and a few others were left standing.

'Now,' the pastor said with renewed confidence. 'All of you that are standing come to the altar and we will pray with you.'

Janet shook her head as she moved slowly out from her seat. The others followed her.

His prayer for them was long, but not as long as Janet had feared. He did not lay hands on them. And in a relatively short time they were standing, facing him, in silence. The hush behind them grew and grew.

The pastor's eyes moved slowly over them, '. . . Is there any among you that would like to turn your back on sin and give your heart to the Lord? You heard the song, "This world is not our home. We're just passing through".'

Janet looked down at the floor.

'Jesus is waiting patiently. Please raise your hand if you want to give your heart to the lord.' He stopped and looked at them in turn.

'. . . It may be your last chance . . . There is only one thing certain about life, and that is death . . . The Lord has already payed for that home in heaven with the sweat and blood that He shed on Calvary's mount . . . Oh yes my friends . . . There is nothing you have to do except come to Him. Where will *you* spend your eternity? Where will your home be for those endless ages? In that home or in hell fire . . . ?'

Janet squeezed her toes inside her shoes, embarrassed, as he broke down again. She couldn't take more of his crying. The heat rose in her body. She looked up and met his eyes.

'Will you not give him your heart? He is pleading with you. Can you not see Him on the cross dying for you? The blood running down from His hands . . . His feet . . . side . . . All for a *wretched* sinner like you?'

Janet's anger rose with the heat.

His eyes, red with pained concentration served only to incense her more. Their eyes held. Janet feared the whole church saw them glaring at each other. She shook her head long enough for it to register with him, turned, and went back to her seat.

The other unsaved took their cue from her and turned away too. When he spoke again they were all sitting down. A sharp silence echoed around his empty words.

For the first time in her life Janet felt victory over him.

Twenty-one

Janet slammed the car door and slumped into the seat.

Joy turned on the engine, slid the car into first gear and pulled away from the church. It seemed much longer than three hours since they had arrived.

'Nobody has changed,' Janet spoke very quietly, a resigned finality in her voice. 'It's as if life has been standing still since I left.'

Joy could see only a bit of her face in the mirror and she tried to avoid even that.

Esmine turned and tried to smile at her, but her own lips had become too rigid. She sat sideways so she could see her friend.

'He is the worst . . . I suppose he can't help it.' Janet's voice was so quiet she might have been talking to herself. 'Joy, will you turn left at the end of the road please? There's a playground at the end. Can we sit in it for a while? They won't be getting home yet . . . They have tea and biscuits and they'll talk.'

'Fine,' Joy answered, weighed down with guilt.

Janet's voice remained heavy and detached, 'I suppose I should understand. If you preach to others and tell them you are led by God and you want to lead them to God, and your own children are backsliders . . .'

Esmine reached out to her, 'Jan don't upset yourself.'

She continued as if she hadn't heard, 'It must be awful for them... for him to have his only daughter turn out like me. A wreck! Who

164

can blame him for saying that she's possessed by seven devils?'

Esmine showed her anger then. 'Don't take that on, Janet. That was disgraceful!'

Joy cleared her throat, but could find nothing to add.

They parked and found a bench facing the children's play area.

As soon as they sat down Janet started talking again. 'Did you see the look on his face when he asked for those who were saved to sit down, and I continued to stand?'

Esmine and Joy shook their heads.

'If the floor could have opened and taken him in he would have welcomed it. I think he hoped I would sit down and admit to him privately that I had backslided. It was as if I'd slapped him in the face.'

She pressed her hands between her legs, her eyes staring blankly at the fenced-in children who charged madly, from roundabout to swing to slide to sandpit.

The three women arrived at the house just seconds before the pastor and his wife. They stood up as he came into the sitting room.

Sister Murray smiled uneasily at them. 'Young ladies, come through to the kitchen. Sam will want to relax a bit.'

The pastor took off his jacket and handed it to his wife as she left the room.

Joy watched him carefully avoiding Janet's eyes.

Janet was looking down at her hands.

They followed Sister Murray back into the hall. She shut the door behind her. 'Oh Janet, God be praised.' She embraced her daughter.

'Mother, please.' Janet tried to pull away.

Her mother backed off, hurt written all over her face. Joy's heart went out to her.

'Come on, let me show you into the dining room. I'll go up and change into my house frock and get the dinner ready.'

They followed her obediently.

Joy longed to tell Janet to go upstairs with her mother, but she had done enough harm already. She kept her mouth firmly closed.

Soon Sister Murray was back, busying herself with the rice and peas and chicken and chatting about her sons.

'I don't know, I hardly see those boys. The last time I saw them was yesterday but I suppose they'll drag their dead selves in sooner or later.' Her eyes lingered on Janet.

Joy could bear it no longer. Brushing aside Sister Murray's objections she got up to help her prepare the food, chatting loudly about nothing at all.

Janet and Esmine sat in virtual silence.

'Are you girls going to stay for night's service?' Sister Murray looked hopefully at Joy.

But Janet leapt in, 'Mum you know we have to go back after dinner. Joy and Esmine are going to work tomorrow.'

'I see.' Her mother's face dropped.

Eventually the table was set, the dinner placed on it, and it was time to call the pastor. He blessed the table and sat down.

Everyone ate in silence until the pastor spoke. 'Were you girls brought up in the Church?' He put his fork down and looked from Joy to Esmine.

Joy looked closely at him before she answered, wondering whether he ever smiled, whether he ever spoke about anything other than Church and saving grace.

'Our parents were Anglican. At least our mother was.'

'I see.' He picked up his knife and fork and continued with his meal.

Joy was just about to test her theory on him by asking him about his childhood in Jamaica, when he put his cutlery down and spoke again, 'Your parents were the ones who were killed so tragically weren't they?'

'Yes,' Joy said simply, carefully avoiding her sister's eyes.

'Life is so unpredictable. As I was saying in my sermon this morning, the only thing certain about life is death!'

Janet's sigh was long and audible. She touched her mother's arm, hoping she would stop him.

But Sister Murray could only smile weakly.

'. . . Most people live from day to day, taking pride in their jobs or in their education, the material things of life, and forget about death until it comes and steals them away.'

Janet shifted uneasily in her seat, biting on her tongue until she felt the salty taste of blood.

'Dad, do you always have to be so morbid? I don't see why you have to talk about death . . .' She spoke without thinking.

It seemed to be the cue he had been waiting for, 'I knew you wouldn't see. You saw once. Don't be proud that you don't see now.' He spoke, not looking at her, his face swelling like a vexed frog.

Suddenly he changed the subject. 'So, you have no intention of coming back home?'

Janet was clearly taken aback for a moment. She sighed but didn't answer.

He didn't seem to notice her exasperation. 'I thought you would have learnt by now that you will never win this game you're playing.'

Silence.

Sister Murray shuffled in her chair and cleared her throat.

'You're staying in London being a burden to complete strangers. You know what you have to do to get your place back in this house.'

'Jan is no burden Pastor . . . Mr Murray.' Joy used the most impatient tone she could muster.

'I am not Mr Murray. I am Pastor to you.'

Esmine lifted one eyebrow and fingered her earrings. Joy's eyes widened.

167

He turned his attention back to his daughter, '. . . God has been too patient with you. If He was like man . . .'

'If he was like you, you mean . . .' Janet shot him an accusing look. The pastor's bottom lip shook with anger as Janet met and held his eyes.

Sister Murray tried desperately to distract her daughter. 'Janet dear . . .'

'Talk to him!' Janet snapped.

'I certainly hope you are not referring to me as *him*. You are not in you den of iniquity now . . . in your harlot house . . . You are in the house of God!'

'Mr Murray!' Joy's fingers were on her chin, her eyes wide with fury.

Esmine cleared her throat hard. 'Joy,' she whispered angrily, 'say Pastor for goodness sake. Don't make it worse.'

'*Mr* Murray,' Joy emphasised, holding his eyes. 'I think that's appalling. You really shouldn't . . .'

'Young lady, I would thank you to refrain from telling me what I should or should not think. This is not a matter for strangers, and you are in my house . . .'

'Sam, don't upset yourself . . .' Sister Murray stood up and raised her hands, '. . . Oh father in heaven I pray for peace . . .'

'Peace? Peace!' her husband thundered. '. . . How can there be peace when Satan reigns in our midst?'

Joy's mouth fell open. Janet started to cry.

'Take one of the serviettes and wipe your face! I tell you, no amount of that slobbering will make me hold my tongue. It is better that you fall into my hands now than later into the hands of God.'

Joy shouted, 'This is disgraceful . . .'

Esmine pushed her chair back and got up, holding her hand out to Janet, 'Come, let's go up to the bathroom. Come . . .'

Janet stood up.

Esmine rested her eyes on the pastor long enough for him to feel the heat of her contempt before directing her friend out of the room.

Joy turned words and phrases around in her mind, finding none that she could utter. None came that she would not later regret. If he had not been Janet's father, if the situation was not already as bad as it could be, if Sister Murray had not been there, she might have used one or two of them. It was not like her to think before she spoke, but she forced the bitter words back.

Sister Murray got up, her plump red skin glowing. In her confusion she hovered, walked down into the kitchen before she remembered that she was intending to clear the table.

Joy got up hastily, 'I'll help you clear up Sister Murray.'

'Thank you dear.' She turned around full circle, twice, and walked into the kitchen like a bird on burning sand.

Eventually the clearing up was done, and Joy climbed the stairs tremulously to see how Janet was. Sister Murrary followed.

Janet was sitting glumly on her old bed, made up as if the room was waiting for her. Her mother attempted to hug her.

'My dear, I'm sorry about all that. But what can I do?'

Janet stiffened and pulled away.

'Janet, please bear with him . . . with me. Don't let this stop you from coming . . . One day you'll want to come back home . . .' She burst into tears. Joy watched Janet's indecision. She seemed to waiver between touching her mother and recoiling. Finally she moved right away from her and sat down alone.

Joy sat with Sister Murray, rubbing her back until she was calm again.

As they left, Janet called out goodbye to her father. He came out, his face set, to speak to her.

'Remember what I said to you,' was all he would say before turning his attention to Joy and Esmine. 'God bles you. I will remember you in my prayers. God knows my prayers are needed.'

He shook his head solemnly, turned and went back to the sitting room.

Sister Murray squeezed her hands together apologetically. 'He was preparing his message for the night service . . . He doesn't like to leave it once he starts . . .'

Janet allowed her mother then to hug her briefly, but she couldn't return the affectionate pressure.

Sister Murray, defeated, kissed Joy and Esmine loudly on their mouths. 'Thank you girls for bringing Janet up . . .'

Janet was already leading the way to the car.

Calling after her, her mother said, '. . . Janet, I hope you can find it in your heart to come back. Don't let me suffer because of . . .' She trailed off.

Joy hugged her, knowing that however hard she pressed their bodies together, she could not be a substitute for Janet.

When Joy looked back at Sister Murray standing by herself at the gate, it struck her that she had never seen anyone looking so lost and homeless outside their own home.

Twenty-two

That night Janet dreamt, and when she woke her disappointment was bitter. She tried to get back to sleep and take up where she had left off but she couldn't. So instead she went over the dream in her mind until she could feel its warmth again and savour its sweetness.

She didn't know how she had got there, but she had found herself in a room. She looked fabulous. Felt wonderful. Gone was the washed-out look, the hollow, gaunt face. Her skin had glowed, like ripened melon. And her eyes had taken on a greyness, not like her father's, but one that was warm, like the sea in the Caribbean at dusk.

All around the room were mirrors. It had once been used for training dancers.

There were only women in the room, all seated in a circle around a pool. Janet was not afraid.

It must have been summer because they were wearing the scantiest of clothes. Chiffon. The wind swept through the opened windows, sucked the clothes into their waists and played with their hems.

They were free, happy with their bodies. They laughed with the wind and made eyes at themselves.

Then Janet realised that they were waiting for her. She rose slowly to her feet. The women cheered and nodded, making eyes at

171

her, laughing not with the wind now but with her.

They stood and reached out for her, touched her.

Moving through the circle she made them stand up. Walking behind the first, she embraced her from behind, in front of the next one, she embraced her too. And so it went on. She was weaving in and out of the circle faster and faster until she was dancing with them. Just touching. Touching and moving away. Running her hands up the legs of one then another. Feeling flesh against chiffon. Her lips parting and trembling.

Moving from the ecstasy of their skin, she found herself bathing in the pool of clear water, the ripples of their laughter around her.

Janet switched on the light, her heart still racing. Running her hand down her body she found it came away wet. She threw off the duvet, but feeling the chill of spring she pulled the cover over her again. Why did I have to wake up?

As she tried to recapture the details of the dream the memory of the day before crept up on her, erasing what remnants of pleasure remained. Embarrassment and shame overwhelmed her. What *would* Esmine and Joy have thought of her family? She pulled the duvet over her head, burrowing further under it, but to no avail. There was no hiding from the humiliation she felt.

Eventually she got out of bed, determined to do something positive. Leaving the house, she walked purposefully along the high street. She knew she should try for another temporary job but her legs wouldn't carry her into the employment agency. She walked past it several times, averting her face, fearing they would recognise her.

Accepting eventually that she wasn't ready to resume the search for work that day, she forced herself to take the bus to Putney, to see if she could walk by the river alone without being afraid.

She walked along the bank that led to the sailing club, feeling nothing, beginning to wonder why she had ever been afraid. Her eyes drifted constantly to the water as she walked. If anything, she felt enlivened by the fresh breeze, the seagulls, the stillness.

The people passing did not recoil and stare at her as she had imagined they would. She found herself wondering what it would be like to be inside their bodies – normal individuals out for a stroll, no tortured history to burden them.

She felt herself envying them because they had fathers who had gone to the park with them, who had held their hands, talked with them, fathers who would tell them off, at home or in the park and not from the lofty height of a pulpit; fathers who smiled because they were not perpetually striving to attain the heavenly home.

Janet reached the sailing club and turned round, feeling strangely calm and very reluctant to return to the house. She sat on a bench next to an elderly white man. He won't want to speak to me, she thought.

She was wrong. He spoke almost as soon as she sat down.

'Nice day.'

Janet looked round in surprise. There was no one else in earshot. She ignored him. Perhaps he's speaking to himself.

'Are you from Africa?' He turned to look in her general direction.

Janet frowned. *Why Africa? Must be crazy.* She looked at him briefly and shook her head. *Perhaps if I don't answer he'll leave me alone.*

'I lived in Africa for years you know. Lovely country it was then. Not the same since they took over, you understand.'

Janet sat up. *Who the hell does he think he is? Trust me to choose to sit here. Typical.* She moved over to the edge of the seat. *Give it a few more minutes and then I'll get up. Better the traffic than this.*

'Kenya.'

'Sorry?' She made a face and held her body further away from him.

'I lived in Kenya.'

'I see.' *The last thing I want now is for this man to unburden on me. Find Kipling's grave.*

173

'Like the river do you?'

Thank God he has left Africa. I don't need anything else to make me angry.
'Yes.'

'I come here every day. Now that I'm on the scrap there is little else I can do.'

'I see.' She looked fully at him. His tone touched something in her.

'Old people don't have any place in this society. I have my strength. I could still work, but they made me redundant. I was only sixty.'

'Oh dear.' Then, 'I'm sorry.'

He didn't seem to hear her.

'I say, you speak with a very, what shall I say? A nice English accent.'

Janet shook her head.

'You have been here a long time then?'

Janet looked at him with pity.

His eyes were still on the river.

'I was born in London . . .' She stopped herself, wondering why she had to explain anything to him. But for some reason she thought of what Esmine might have said, of how outraged she would have been if he had said that to her. 'Why do you people always assume that we have come from somewhere else? I'm British, like you.'

He turned then and looked at her, 'I see, equal rights and all that.'

'Sorry?' Perhaps he's hard of hearing. I really should just ignore him.

'I won't ever get used to it. No offence meant, mind you. England for the Englishman for me.'

Janet changed her mind. She couldn't let him get away with that. 'What are you going to do with all the women?'

'Don't follow you my dear, what women?'

'You said "England for the Englishman". Where are you going to put the other half of the population, the women?'

He laughed, a hearty laugh. It changed his whole face. He looked almost sincere, almost human, Janet thought. She found his laugh infectious. She smiled and then suddenly realised that she had never seen an old white man smile, let alone laugh. It made her sorry and sad.

'There is so much new thinking these days. I see so few people. So few. Everybody ignores you. If they think you're going to talk, they bury their heads and hurry past or shout some patronising comment at you. They always think you're deaf.'

'I'm sorry,' Janet said, remembering guiltily that this was what she too had thought.

'For what dear? Nothing to apologise for. You've made my day. You made me laugh, something I haven't done in months.'

She felt an overwhelming sadness for him. But sadness she could do without.

She stood up to go. 'I have to go now.'

He stood up, held out his hand.

She shook it firmly.

'Goodbye now.' He looked fully into her face. 'I say, you have grey eyes. How unusual.'

Janet smiled. 'Bye. Take care.'

'Good day to you my dear.'

Janet looked back at him a few times before she turned on to the road.

Even a white man who used to live in Kenya and thinks I speak with an English accent, laughed with me and took hold of my hand . . . And those women in my dreams desired me . . . So I can't be all that bad. There can't be anything wrong with me. She looked down at her feet. Was she skipping or was that in her mind too? She didn't know, but she smiled fully as she crossed the road to get the bus home.

Twenty-three

      It was Esmine's day to cook so it promised to be something simple. She stood with her back to the kitchen sink.

Janet stood watching her, sipping cold tea.

'You don't think Joy will mind pasta and a sauce do you Jan?'

Janet smiled and rested the tea on the surface beside her, feeling light and relaxed after her afternoon by the river. 'She's going to complain.'

Esmine knew Janet was right. On her day, Joy always made an effort doing two or three courses. Esmine made a face, 'I know, but I can't be bothered.'

'I'll make something else?' Janet offered.

'You sure?'

'Ummm.'

Esmine walked across the room and opened one of the cupboards, 'What though?'

Janet looked in the fridge, 'There's okkra. I'll do something with that?'

Esmine nodded, 'We have onions. Let me see, what else? Tuna and green peppers?'

'That'll be all right.'

'Oh great Jan. Ta . . . You've saved me an earful about who makes what effort.'

'I'll do the okkra first and then you can do the pasta when it's simmering.'

'Fine.' Esmine moved across and leaned on the fridge. 'So yesterday is over and today is a new day.' She smiled, a worried look on her face, 'Feel a bit better now?'

'Yes. I think I do.'

'Actually you do look better.'

'I went to Putney and I talked to an old white man and he made me laugh . . .' She stopped, hearing her voice. It didn't sound like her, more like a four-year-old waking up on her birthday.

Esmine smiled, more surprised than relieved. 'Well, if an old man brings that kind of excitement out in you, I would love to see what a young one would do.'

'You sound like Joy!'

'I know . . . speaking of whom, whatever you do, don't tell her. She'll go looking for him.'

'He's the wrong colour . . .'

'That's true.'

Janet cut the ends off the okkra, washed them and put them to steam.

'I'll open the tuna and chop the onions for you.'

'Ta.'

'Your mother is a good cook.'

Janet stopped what she was doing and looked away, 'I was so angry with her yesterday.'

'I know . . .'

'She's still there, letting Dad turn her round like a top, confusing her.'

'She's torn isn't she?'

'Yes. She wants peace, as she's always saying. And she gets it, but at what cost?'

'Do you think she's unhappy?'

Janet used the knife to play with the chopped onions. 'I don't know really, it's hard to tell.'

'She looks well though Jan. I suppose all those women in the church look well. None of them look haggard.'

'Yes. Grace.'

'What?'

'Grace. That's what Mum would say. The grace of God . . . That's what keeps them young.'

She took out a frying pan, tipped oil in it, stirred in the onions and green peppers.

'Are you still angry with her Jan?' Esmine asked gently.

'No . . . I don't suppose there's any point. I just feel sorry for her.' She stirred the contents of the frying pay absent-mindedly. 'She's so weak. She's never been a person separate from my father.' She sighed heavily. 'She's never known where *she* is going, and she holds no influence over him. She lets him lead her all the time, even if she knows he's wrong.' Janet shook her head. 'She never makes him listen to her . . . never . . . How can you respect a woman like that?'

Esmine saw a picture of her own mother, so unlike that.

'What will you do? She's desperate for you to forgive her, to go back home.'

'Never!'

Esmine fingered her earring, taken aback by her friend's vehemence.

'Let me have the tuna please, Esmine, and perhaps a tin of tomatoes too.' Esmine got the tin, opened it and passed it to her.

'That will be ready in about ten minutes. Oh goodness, garlic, seasoning! Can you get them?'

Esmine handed them over. 'That smells nice Jan. Thanks.'

'I used to like cooking . . .'

'I hate it. As you know, I hate every possible thing about keeping a house. And contrary to what that sister of mine says, it has nothing to do with my nails. I just hate it.'

'You'll find somebody who will do it all for you.'

'But what would I have to do for him?' She got up. 'Oh well, I'll put the pasta on . . .' Then, 'Jan, do you regret going yesterday? Joy was feeling really guilty.'

'Not now. I did when I sat in church . . . and when we were at the table . . . even when I woke up this morning. But as the day wore on, I knew it had helped me to make one decision.'

Esmine ran the wooden spoon through the bubbling pasta and turned to face her. 'Yes? What's that?'

Janet ran her fingers across her mouth. 'Up to yesterday I always felt that I had no choice, that I would eventually have to go back there one day . . . that I needed to. That it all came in a package. Home with them. Church. Home in heaven at the end . . . Happiness.' She shook her head.

Esmine smiled encouragement.

'I felt that I needed that kind of security. I knew that with them there would be no freedom, that I would never be able to be myself. But still I felt that was what I had to do. Even after talking about it again and again to Anita. I felt that I'd go back eventually. But seeing them, him especially, I know, I know that I could never go back there . . .'

'But Esmine, your mother . . .'

Janet sighed. 'I don't mean never go and see her. I feel a bit awful about the way I treated her yesterday. So I will go back for her . . . to make up to her . . .'

'When?'

'I haven't decided yet, but I will. Soon. I even want to talk to *him*. To say my piece once and for all . . . That will be the next step up the mountain for me.'

'What mountain?'

'Joy told me that your dad used to compare life with climbing a mountain.'

Esmine smiled, 'Yes . . .' She ran her spoon through the pasta,

'I'll turn this off now. It smells wonderful Jan. If I wasn't scared of my nose growing I'd tell Joy that I did it.'

'You can if you want.'

'She wouldn't be fooled. She knows me . . . Shall we eat? I'm not going to wait for her.'

They were soon tucking into platefuls of food.

'You know, I *was* awful to Mum yesterday Esmine!' Janet smiled. 'I think I'll call her tonight.'

'That's great,' Esmine replied; 'she'll be happy.'

'I think I'll arrange to go up in a month or so for this talk.'

'Right. Do you want me to go with you?'

'Thanks, but no.' She sighed, 'I have to do it by myself.'

'You sure you'll be all right.'

Janet nodded, 'I'll have to be . . . I have to face it and put it behind me.'

'Then you can start climbing again.'

'Then I can start climbing again.'

When Joy returned home Janet sat with her as she ate. She was anxious to put Joy's mind at rest. She owed Joy too much to let her go on feeling guilty on her account.

'Did you cook, Janet?'

'Did Esmine tell you then?'

Esmine had gone up to have a bath.

'It must be you. Who else would go to the trouble of doing a salad, cooking up okkra and doing a pasta dish all on the same evening?'

'She did the pasta.'

'Thank God for that.' Joy continued eating. She looked extremely tired, Janet thought.

'Joy?'

Joy sipped her mango juice and looked up, 'Still upset?'

'No, as a matter of fact I'm not.'

180

'Oh.'

'I just wanted to say that perhaps . . . I mean in retrospect, it was a good idea to go up there yesterday.'

'I'm glad *you* think so. I've never been so furious in my whole life. I'm sorry Janet, I don't mean to be disrespectful to your father but . . .'

'You don't have to be sorry. I was there too.'

'So why do you think it was a good idea?'

Joy finished eating and pushed her plate aside.

'I think I know now that's not where home is any more. It can never be there.'

'Are you sure?'

'As sure as I can be. It's not even that actual house. I mean the whole area, the whole way of life.' She shook her head. 'You know the funny thing is, if Daddy hadn't taken my keys, if he hadn't harassed me so much and turned up that night, I might have done one or two things that would have displeased him if he knew about them, but in the end I suspect I would have asked forgiveness . . .'

'Of him?' Joy was appalled.

'Oh no, of God. I would have asked forgiveness and gone back home. I would have taken my room back, gone out to work, to church. Stayed like that until I got married, perhaps to a pastor. Most likely to a pastor. Had kids and continued like that until I became another Mummy.'

'Janet, that's the most depressing thing I've ever heard in my life. That is really depressing.'

'It depresses me too now. But I suppose that's how it would have happened. I would have lived with his constantly finding fault with me, with my imperfections. But I would have lived with it.

'He thinks that's his duty, *to prune and prune until the day of harvest*. But I would have worked out a survival strategy, I suppose, like Mum has done. And so it would have gone on until I died and inherited eternal life in the heavenly home.'

'You would have bloody well deserved it.'

Janet smiled at the look of anger on Joy's face.

'If only he knew how close he came.'

'Perhaps he does, hence the anger. What anger! I can't remember ever seeing so much anger in one person, and in *church*.'

'He'd call it zeal.'

'*Really*!' Then, 'So where do you go from here?'

Janet made a face. 'I plan to go in a month. Before you came I was speaking to Mum.'

Joy smiled vacantly at her. 'You know, before I met your mother I didn't understand how much I admired my own.'

'Really?'

'Yes. My father to me was always the one with the power, the insight, the strength, the determination. But I have to admit now that my mother was powerful too.' A sadness came over her face. 'Perhaps it is not just him that I have to thank for everything . . .'

She sighed and looked intently at Janet. 'If you have the inclination to take any more advice from me, make up with your mother Janet. Forgive her . . . Don't let anything happen to her without you doing that . . .'

Twenty-four

It was Joy's favourite time of year. She loved spring in England. She was going to miss it.

Gone were the early nights, the perpetual darkness and gloom, the heavily coated people, their heads buried in collars. Shapeless, faceless people, rushing home.

In spring people walked slower, their heads came up a bit, not much, but enough for you to see that they at least had foreheads, that they saw through eyes and not through the tops of their heads.

Trees came alive.

With a fascination that was almost childlike Joy watched the buds, and then the stalks and branches, come alive with leaves. And the daffodils. And tulips. The glorious yellows and reds. She spent a lot of time dragging Lee or Esmine or Janet for long walks with her through parks.

She was walking with Lee now, the first time in ages that she had found the time to see him.

'I wish I'd planned to go back in spring.'

Lee tightened his grip on her hand but didn't answer.

She wanted to tell him what else was on her mind, that the time was dragging and she was getting fed up with waiting.

'Did you hear me sweetheart?' She felt good and refused to have her spirit dampened.

'Yes. Why?' He sounded anything but interested.

They had parked by the Robin Hood Gate entrance to Richmond Park and were walking towards the ponds.

'Spring always makes me feel good and I would have left with a good feeling.'

'I see.'

I'll leave it, she thought. *I don't want to upset him today, not when the leaves, and the flowers are out. Besides he's been great up to now, I have to give him that.*

She had expected, with her going, with *that* woman around, that their relationship would have deteriorated, that he would have changed. In fact there were times when she had hoped it would. That might have made things easier.

If he had changed and become beastly to her. If he had been selfish. If he had asked her not to go. If he had picked quarrels with her, he would have given her the perfect excuse to end what was left of the relationship, to tell him honestly this time to get the hell out of her life.

When he hadn't done any of those things she had taken to testing him. She had refused to see him when she could have done. Had picked quarrels with him. Had been impatient with him, had ignored him, had often unleashed her greatest weapon, her tongue, against him. But as Lee was Lee, none of that served her warped purpose, merely left her feeling guilty and wretched.

When there were no conflicts he worked with her on her plans, and even at those times she could not bring herself to admit that she might miss him.

She found herself, though, minding very much that there was another woman waiting for him. And even though she told herself that Loretta was not his type, she feared that she could see them together.

Now as that thought came to her, more questions about Loretta, about what he intended to do once she was gone, floated to the tip of her tongue.

She turned the questions over and over in her mind – the exact way to phrase them, the voice she would use, so he would not guess that she was burning up with jealousy and anger. She would not want him to think that she was vulnerable, at least not when she was at her weakest.

She heard the end of something he said. 'Sorry? What was that you said?'

'I was just saying you are miles away.'

She apologised weakly. They got to the pond, and stood looking at the ducks and swans.

After a while they started walking again, along the edge of the pond. Still plagued by uneasiness, she thought of probing him.

'Will you see Esmine and Janet when I've gone? I would really appreciate it if you visited them, just to see how they're getting on . . .'

Lee's smile was crooked, 'So you're worried about them? They *are* adults you know. I'm sure they don't need looking after . . .'

Joy stopped walking. 'Are you saying that you don't want to, that as soon as I go you'll not even bother to see how they are?' She slipped her hand out of his.

Lee shrugged and continued walking.

'Lee, is that what you are saying?' she shouted, her hands akimbo.

He stopped and turned, conscious of the people in earshot.

She was still standing where the conversation had started.

He sighed and walked back reluctantly.

'Are you saying that as soon as I go you'll not even bother to see how they are?'

'I didn't say that.'

'You did. You said they were adults.'

Lee raised his eyes to the cloudy skies.

'I thought you would do that one last thing for me. I thought you cared enough.' She wheeled off and left him standing.

He followed her.

'Joy, what I should have said and what I'm not explaining very well is this . . .'

'Yes, try and wriggle out of it.'

'Joy will you listen please?'

'You know you've never liked my sister or, to put it more precisely, you have never liked our relationship.'

He tutted. 'What's that got to do with anything?' He was getting angry, his voice like sandpaper on glass.

'Let's leave it. I asked you to walk with me because I wanted some peace.'

'You can have it if you stop upsetting yourself.' Then, 'Sweetheart, I didn't intend to stop seeing Esmine. I just don't feel that I need you to make an order.'

'I was not making an order!' She pushed the words out through her teeth, 'I don't know why I bother. I should know that you can't wait for me to leave, to sever all links. I don't know why you just don't stop wasting your time and do it now.'

'I thought that was your game,' he said quietly, looking at her. He stopped, his hands stuffed in his pockets, his eyes full of challenge.

She knew he had stopped but she continued to walk, deciding impulsively to go to the car. She hated being transparent, hated allowing him to feel that he knew her, that he knew her game. She hated the truth when it demeaned her.

She passed the first car park, passed one group of deer, passed another group, to where their car was. It was only then that she remembered he had driven *his* car and had the keys with him.

Oh Christ! She turned then, but he was nowhere in sight. *I'm going to kill him. The creep.* Her sigh came out broken. She rested against the car, watched people buying ice-cream, wondering how they could, when it was so chilly. Still no Lee.

She looked at her watch, furious. He should have got there by now if he'd waited ten minutes and then started to walk. The minutes ticked away. She shook herself to keep warm, determined not to go back to look for him. She felt he would be trying to teach her a lesson, knowing all the time he had the key.

She decided finally that she would buy herself an ice-cream. She hated soft ice-cream but she had to do something with her hands. She had to be doing something when he came. She had to appear relaxed and in control, as if she had just got there. She would pretend that she had gone for a longer walk, that he hadn't kept her waiting for an hour.

She bought the ice-cream with no intention of eating it, turned and saw him coming towards her. Her fury rose. The thought of squashing the ice-cream over his face and rubbing it in crossed her mind. But as he came nearer all she could think of was how beautiful he was, and that there could never be anyone else like him. No one who could move her as he did. Not even in Jamaica.

She moved away from the van and faced him.

'I thought you hated soft ice-cream.' He was smiling but it could have cracked his face; his eyes were sad, his cheeks rigid.

'I do. I hate them, and anyway it's too cold.'

'So why did you buy it?'

'I don't know.'

He took a step back, 'It wasn't by any chance to plaster over my face, was it?'

She half-smiled, shaking her head slowly.

'I'm sorry Lee,' she found herself saying. Then she wanted to apologise for everything else. To spell it out. But she couldn't bring herself to say more. Instead she took a step closer to him, telling him again. 'I *am* really sorry.'

He bent over and licked the ice-cream. Covering her hand with his, he raised the ice-cream to her lips. She tasted it but made a face. He put his left arm around her waist, held her hand up to his mouth as he directed her back to the car, eating the ice-cream as they walked.

Back at the car she leaned against it, his body resting against hers, licking the ice-cream until it was down to the cone. He continued holding her hand as they walked over to the bin to throw away the cone. They turned, she lowered her head on to his shoulder, and they walked back together to the car.

When Joy fell asleep later she dreamt that the horse-chestnut outside her window had been replaced by a cypress. And she watched it, not from her bedroom window now, but from underneath. She stroked the trunk with her naked toes.

They didn't sleep long. They got up and showered and went downstairs.

'Sweetheart,' she murmured.

'Umm.'

'You mustn't get annoyed because I'm not going to say this to make you annoyed, okay?'

'Fine.'

She rubbed her hand over her face. 'I really value what we have had; value what we have. But when I go, I don't want you to stay here and hope against hope . . .'

'And since you have no intention of coming back, and Jamaica is not *my* home . . .'

'I wasn't going to put it exactly like that.'

'But that's what you mean.'

She stroked his face. 'I mean that I want you to be happy.'

He sighed.

She wanted to add, *so long as it is not with Loretta*, but she controlled herself.

He didn't speak and she couldn't think of how to phrase what she meant. The silence hung over them like a cloud.

Twenty-five

       Janet decided that she would go and visit her parents on a Friday morning. The house would be empty. Her mother and brothers would be at work and, most importantly, her father would be out. She had phoned her mother the night before and she had reminded Janet that he would be at his normal counselling sessions at the church, and would not be home until late.

'Oh, my dear, I'm so glad you are coming. So glad, so glad, so glad. We can really talk. I have missed you since you were here ... Your father keeps telling me that I'm foolish ... Anyway I'm really looking forward to seeing you ...'

'Mum,' Janet had interrupted, 'I'm coming to see you and to talk to Dad. I don't know if I want to go to church on Sunday. I'll decide when I get there, okay?' She knew that she had no intention of going.

There was a pause before her mother answered, 'Janet, sweetheart, you know how your father will feel about that. He will take it to heart . . . and the brethren will think you are being disrespectful.'

'Mum, please don't.' What she wanted to say was that she did not care what the brethren thought. Instead she sighed loudly, meaning her mother to hear.

'All right dear, I don't want you to go worrying yourself now.

189

Don't put yourself under any more pressure . . . Mind you, prepare yourself, he will take it hard.'

The coach left Victoria Station on time but arrived later than scheduled. Janet didn't mind. She slept, waking at one stage to find her head resting on the shoulder of the man next to her.

Before she managed to apologise he said, 'Don't worry, Sis. You seem to need your rest, so I didn't want to disturb you.'

Unusually for her, she too saw the funny side. They spent the remainder of the journey talking. It made the time go quickly for her and helped her to forget her nervousness.

When she arrived home she found a note from her mother on the dining table telling her that there was food in the pot on the stove for her. Janet opened the Dutch pot and the saucepan. There was spinach and salt fish in one and plain rice in the other.

Looking for something to calm her, she sought the familiarity of her old room. She could see that her mother had fixed it up for her. The scent was overpowering. It was how she remembered it smelling as a child – of food cooking downstairs mingled with wax furniture polish. She opened one of the windows and sat on the edge of the bed.

The walls were as she had left them. A poster she remembered buying at a youth convention, years before, caught her eye. It promised resurrection for all who are faithful unto death.

She shook her head as a stale feeling of sadness, uncertainty and guilt overpowered her. It was always like that when the memory of those church-filled days came to her. She wasn't sure then whether it was because she missed the certainty that had come with the Sunday services, youth meetings, revival services, conventions and women's retreats, or whether it was because she longed for something else to fill the gaping hole that was left in her now they were gone.

She stretched out on the bed. She had lived and breathed all that.

If she missed a service, like others she would make a public apology in her testimony. Her absences were always caused *by the wiles of the devil*. That was the only excuse *she* had been allowed. For others there was the luxury of their unsaved husbands or simply *circumstances over which they had no control*. Even then she had been jealous of them. But yet she remembered frowning at them, playing God, feeling that they were in *a backslidden condition*, destined to miss out on eternal life.

Janet pushed her shoes off and curled up in the foetal position. But she was unable to sleep. Her throat was dry. She went downstairs, made some tea. On her way back, without thinking, she tried the door of her parents' room.

She was surprised to find it unlocked. She went inside. That room hadn't changed either. Time had stood still there as it had in church and in her own room.

There was the fluffy bedspread that she remembered. It matched the cover on the ottoman, and the curtains, pink and white, her mother's favourite colours. The mantlepiece over the unused fireplace contained the same ornaments, a variety of ceramic pots, plaques with scripture verses, a vase containing stiff plastic flowers.

Janet could not have explained why looking at them caused her to feel that her mother was trapped.

She sat by the dressing table, facing herself in the mirror. Long ago, when her father was out and she had been alone with her mother, she had sometimes sat there. What she could not remember was how she had looked, in the days when people had considered her pretty.

She couldn't bear to see herself so she left the room, closing the door tightly behind her as in the past. She would not want her father to know that she had been there.

She went back downstairs, not knowing how to relax.

She went into the sitting room, kicking off her shoes as she curled up on the settee, where she twisted and turned until she fell asleep.

Janet woke to find her mother standing over her.

'Hello Mum.' She sat up and rubbed her eyes, trying to forget the last time they had met. She had vowed to start afresh, to give her mother a chance.

Her mother bent and kissed her on the mouth. 'You are tired. Go back to sleep . . .'

Janet sat up, not quite able to look at her mother. 'I'm all right now.'

She felt her mother's eyes on her.

'What's wrong?' She asked defensively.

'Girl you look so thin. I don't think you're eating. You didn't see the food I left.'

Janet got up. 'I wasn't hungry.'

Her mother shook her head and took hold of her daughter around the waist, pressing her hands into her sides.

Janet didn't protest.

'You are skin and bone, child, and you used to have such a healthy body . . .' She groaned, 'I noticed when you were here last month you just picked around the food . . . Anyway, this weekend I'll see that you get some good food down you.' She took off her jacket. 'How you two friends? . . . Those girls are nice . . . Well brought up. If only . . .'

'They would give their hearts to the Lord.'

Her mother looked at her, sighed, and started to walk out of the room, mumbling as if to herself, 'All I ask is that you be careful when your father comes home . . . You know how he would feel . . . if he hears you talking like that.'

'I haven't said anything wrong. I knew what you were going to say, that's all.' She followed her mother out of the room.

'I'm going to take my clothes off.'

'I'll come up with you . . . Mum?'

'Yes love.' She stopped half-way up the steps and turned.

'It's good to see you again.'

'Child, I can't tell you how my heart is overflowing. Bless the Lord . . . He has answered my prayers . . .'

Janet sighed very quietly, so her mother couldn't hear.

Back downstairs Janet sat in the dining room as her mother cooked. She was unable to relax. Each time she thought of her father's arrival home, she tensed.

In London she was able to push her feelings about him to the back of her mind. Now in his house she had to face them.

As a child she had not considered the option of not loving him as she had always done her mother. It was how it had to be. Children had to love and honour their parents. Especially if their father was their overseer and pastor.

'Janet you are deep in thought. Let me make you a cup of tea.' Her mother came into the dining room.

Janet stood up. 'I'll do it.'

'No! Sit down. I am going to pamper you this weekend.' Then, looking at her daughter with a sadness Janet had earlier noticed in her eyes. 'I have so much to make up for . . . Two years of love and neglect of my one daughter.'

Simon, Janet's eldest brother, arrived home first, followed soon after by Luke.

'You don't look half as bad as I expected you to . . .' said Simon as he hugged her.

'Thanks,' Janet said with a wry smile.

Their mother came into the dining room, 'Listen, I am going to say it now because I know what you two are like, especially you Simon. I am not going to have you put Janet under any pressure now. You'll have more than enough time tomorrow to speak to her.'

'All right Mum, don't get worked up. We won't hurt the prodigal daughter,' Luke said, looking to Simon for support.

'At least you remember something from the Holy Scriptures,' his mother replied.

Janet talked to them as their mother set the table and brought the food out.

'We are not going to wait for your father. He won't be home until God knows when . . .'

Simon looked up at her, 'Mum, are you sure Dad hasn't got another woman?'

'Simon! I ask you father to take this child,' she said, raising her hands to the ceiling.

'Dad would have a fit if he heard you talking like that,' Janet said, shocked at how her two older brothers had changed – not going to church anymore and now wondering if the pastor had a woman on the side.

'You don't think he has, do you Simon? I'm suspicious too,' Luke laughed.

'Simon and Luke, I forbid you to talk in that disrespectful way about your father . . . You know your father is a man of God.'

Janet coughed. She was liking the new freedom in the house. She suspected though that it only existed in the absence of her father.

As they ate, her mother fussed around her, piling more and more food on her plate. Janet ate more than she would allow herself normally. But her mother was still not satisfied, 'Janet why you picking around the food like that? Eat child or the wind soon blow you way.'

'I'm stuffed Mum.' She put her cutlery down.

Her mother sighed and continued eating.

Simon grinned. 'Jan, tell me something. How about that boy who Dad caught in your arms, him still calling on you?' he asked with a mischievous look.

'Simon!' His mother's tone was emphatic, 'Why do you always

bring the level of the conversation down in the gutters? You are getting from bad to worse.'

'It's all right Mum, I don't mind. No, he's not,' she replied simply, feeling her mother's eyes on her.

' 'How about those two girls you live with then?' Simon turned to Luke and winked.

'You mean women, don't you Simon?'

'Okay, women then. They have boyfriends? I met one of the boys from church after you came up last month. He told me that the guys in the church couldn't take their eyes off them, especially the really tall one . . .'

'Simon! I do not believe the boys from the church said that.' His mother put her hands on her hips.

'Yes Mum, I heard that too,' Luke supported.

'Simon and Luke, I am not going to tell you again, I do not want any of your loose talk at the dinner table.'

'I'm only expressing natural appreciation!'

'For your information,' said Janet, 'they, at least Joy, is taken, and she won't be in England much longer anyway.'

Simon made to continue but was cut short by his mother. 'Janet! Do not encourage them. Those girls, from what I can see, wouldn't be interested in boys like you anyway. They must want boys with ambition. I am going to clear the table and I want to speak to Janet alone afterwards.' She pouted and got up.

But when she came back into the room, she stood for a moment watching her three children chatting and laughing together. She smiled to herself and started to hum a chorus that had been on her mind all day.

Twenty-six

'Girl,' Janet's mother said, sitting heavily on the settee next to her, 'I can't tell how glad I am to have you under this roof again.' She turned and looked briefly at her daughter, 'When your brothers came and we were all sitting at the dining table, I felt better than I have felt for a long time . . . All my children sitting together with me . . . It's a pity your father was not there to enjoy it too.'

Janet didn't want to say she wasn't sure her father would have shared her feeling.

'How does Dad feel about Simon and Luke not going to church?' she asked instead.

'He feels it. I tell him that it's not he who saves and so he should leave it in the hands of God, but it doesn't have much effect. He says when he stands up in church to invite others to God, he sees his own children in front of him and he is sure that the brethren see the three of you too . . .' She shook her head, 'Many nights I wake up to find him on his knees by the bedside, crying and praying for the three of you . . . Oh my dear child, sometimes I feel such a burden. I wish that the three of you could be saved again . . .'

Janet hoped this wouldn't go on. 'Oh Mum, don't take it on . . .' She sighed.

Her mother pressed the palms of her hands together. 'Since you came up last time, after not seeing you for so long, I have been trying to look at things more fully.' She sank deeper into the seat.

Janet watched her.

'I talked to your father about it. I told him that we brought you into the world but we have to let go and let you find your own way.' She stopped and thought for a while. 'But God knows I do not want any of you to go to hell.' She made a face and pressed her fingers into her lips. 'So I can never be complacent. Until you reclaim your first love I will pray for you and the boys night and day.'

'If that makes you happy, Mum, but don't let it make you ill. It won't help.'

'But your souls are so precious to me. I don't want you to be lost.'

Janet listened to her mother's shallow breathing and watched her worried expression, fervently wishing she could take her away from the unrelenting pressure and burden for souls, the midnight weeping and wailing of her father.

Sister Murray shifted in her chair and turned back to her daughter. 'Janet, I have to say this before you go back. I would not like anything to happen to me. I would not like to go my graves without making things right. I am sorry for not being a good mother . . .'

'Mum, you have always . . .' not knowing why she was saying that because she had not believed it for so long.

'Janet, please hear me out.' The lines on her face deepened.

Janet took her mother's hand. Seeing her pain, the unease she had felt with her disappeared. She stroked the back of her mother's hand gently, then kissed her. It occurred to Janet at that moment that she was truly indebted to Esmine and Joy. It was from them that she had learnt that it was possible to speak without using words.

Her mother rested her other hand on top of her daughter's. '. . . I am a grown woman and I have sat all this time not doing what I know I should have done . . . I have sat doing what your father thought was right. Don't get me wrong; I am not blaming him, he didn't force me. I could have done the right thing and still kept peace in the house, kept peace with him. If I had been wise. If I had been strong . . .

'I have prayed for God to forgive me, to forgive me for sitting here when I should have been sitting with you. When I should have been with you holding your hand. I have sat here harbouring the pain in my heart.' She looked deeply into Janet's face.

Janet tried to smile at her but couldn't.

She continued speaking very quietly, 'There would have been no pain if I had simply got up and gone to you when you needed me. I should have been with you, letting you know that I didn't stop loving you . . . Instead I sat here doing nothing when all the time you were suffering.'

She looked away from Janet as the tears welled up in her eyes. Janet rested her hands on her mother's lap. She didn't know what to say. Her mother tried to speak again but started to sob, quietly at first and then loudly, rocking her body as she wept.

Janet had only ever heard her mother cry like that when she had tarried over souls at the altar, and when she had been moved by the spirit.

Janet rested her head on her shoulder.

'If you can only tell me that you forgive me, then perhaps I can begin to forgive myself, begin to ease the pain that is tearing me apart.'

'Oh Mum.'

Since the day they had broken into her flat, Janet had prayed for this day. She had planned it all, planned how much she would tell her parents. That they were hypocrites. That they shouldn't bother to go to church. That God would never forgive them. That even if He did, *she* never would. That she would meet them in hell. And if somehow she managed to escape hell and they didn't, she would be to them as Lazarus had been to Dives – she would watch them burn without stretching out a drop of water to save them.

Now, with her mother's shoulders convulsing and the lines of an old woman etched on her face, Janet knew that she would never say those things.

'Dear, do you forgive me? I need your forgiveness. I beg you to forgive me.'

'Mum, I forgive you.' There! It was out and she wanted to say more, to speak with more conviction in her voice, but other words would not come out although she wanted so much to ease her mother's pain. She drew closer to her and pressed her body to her mother. Somehow she knew that the gulf that had always separated them had now closed, and that they would never again be as they were.

Later, when she was going up for her bath, Janet told her mother that she would not wait up until her father came home. She told herself that she wanted to savour those moments when her mother was in her arms, and that there would be time enough in the morning to face him.

'I'll come up and wash your back,' her mother offered as she mounted the steps behind her.

Janet smiled. She had hoped her mother would offer.

She watched as Janet undressed, shaking her head periodically. 'I was right. You are skin and bone. One thing though, your skin is still as soft as before.' She ran her hands over Janet's back.

Janet got in the bath and turned round so that her back was to her mother. The soft gentle pressure she applied with the sponge soothed Janet.

'That feels really nice Mum . . .' A lump came into her throat.

After her mother had finished and before Janet turned to face her, she dunked her face in the water so that her mother would not see her tears.

The next morning her mother brought her tea in bed. Janet gulped it quickly. She knew that her father would be downstairs and that she might as well face him now.

When her mother left for the shops, Janet went downstairs. She found him in the kitchen finishing off his breakfast.

'Good morning Dad.' She mustered all the cheer she could. It made her voice high-pitched, false, she thought.

He barely opened his mouth. 'Good morning Janet. I was hoping that you would have joined your mother and me for family worship this morning.' His voice was dry.

She cleared her throat. She had not expected that so soon. She shifted from one leg to the next, amazed that standing in his presence alone reduced her to such a feeling of unworthiness.

He still seemed so *big*.

He continued eating, not looking up.

She watched him, afraid to move to the kitchen without being dismissed. She tried again. 'Where are Simon and Luke Dad?'

'Luke went shopping with your mother and Simon says he is working today . . . but you can never tell with that boy.'

'More tea, Dad?'

'Thanks! I'll go up to the living room. You can bring it when you've had your breakfast.' He pushed his plate aside and got up, avoiding her eyes.

She found him reading the Bible. He put it on the seat next to him as she handed him the tea.

'I'm sorry I didn't stay up to see you last night, but I was very tired.' She felt she was trying as hard as she could.

'Your mother told me,' he replied dryly.

She sat on the settee on the opposite side of the room from him.

'Your mother tells me that you are not staying for service tomorrow.' He looked down at the open Bible next to him.

She swallowed before answering, 'I didn't think in my situation . . .'

'And what situation is that?'

She honestly didn't know what situation she meant, so she didn't reply.

When he spoke again his voice was laced with impatience, 'You may have given up on God but He has not given up on you.'

She bit her lips.

'I know that, Dad, but if I had been staying I wouldn't have . . . I couldn't have taken an active part in the service again.'

He looked up, startled.

'Janet!'

She remembered his calling her name in that way when she was a child.

'I did not have the opportunity to ask you this last time you came . . .'

She watched him take the Bible up, look at the open page, close it and return it to the seat. Her nails dug into the back of her hand.

'What led you to backslide?' he asked evenly, straightening his back. '*Are* you living in sin in London. Are you still committing yourself?'

He cleared his throat.

She didn't know whether she should laugh or cry.

'What *do* you mean Dad?' She was trying hard to keep calm.

'Janet! Do not play games with me. You used to know what that meant. I know what I saw in London.' His nostrils flared with his eyes. 'When I came that night, you were in the process of committing yourself . . .'

'That is not true!' She had meant to be calm, to lead the conversation, to say her piece and then go back to her room to wait for her mother.

'Are you calling me a liar, girl? You were in the process of giving your body to that boy. What else would you call it when you were wrapped up on the settee with him?'

She did not answer.

He looked her over with scorn and disgust. 'You have to acknowledge your sins and be washed in the blood of the lamb. Nothing else will heal you broken body.'

Janet closed her eyes for a second. She reminded herself that she should not be surprised by his words. She had learnt as a child that the unnamed act was a sin for both men and women, but that it was a worse sin for women than it could ever be for men. Once committed, it was only women who would be soiled. It was women who would be broken. Once soiled and broken, once the temple of God had been defiled, no amount of secret prayer and repentance would mend her again. Nothing could ever make her clean and whole again, except the blood of the lamb.

Janet suddenly knew that she didn't believe any of that any more. And, what was more, she didn't know why she had ever believed it. Then she realised with a start that she was not cowering under the glare that her father now turned on her. She did not feel that she should rush out and bury herself in sackcloth and ashes in order to feel worthy to stand again in his presence.

So she met his gaze with confidence. *Now that he has said that*, she thought, *he has nothing more to say*. He had used his only ammunition and he had not frightened or intimidated her.

'Dad, with due respect, it is up to you to believe what you want. If I tell you the truth you will not believe me. If I tell you a lie you will not believe me either. I can't win. The only thing that I will say again is that you should remember that I am your daughter, and I think that should be the most important thing to you.'

Her father kept his gaze on her, his expression unchanged. In one sense, Janet thought, as she continued to hold his eyes, she was glad that he was the same. He had not changed since she had known him, the circumstances of their estrangement had made no difference, her illness had made no difference. At least, she thought, he is predictable.

As she watched him, speaking at her, making no apology for

what had happened, feeling no regret, she felt vindicated. She no longer had to pretend to feel what she had never felt. She could admit to herself that she had never loved him. And she would never let that make her feel guilty again.

He looked hard at her, 'As I said before, I can only leave you in the hands of God. But I will thank you not to tell me what should or should not be important to me.' He shifted his gaze from her to his Bible, picked it up without opening it.

As if to appease him, to call a truce, now that she had settled it with herself, she offered him another cup of tea.

'No. Thank you. I have had enough.' He opened his Bible, picked up his glasses and put them on. The signal that their conversation was finished.

Janet relaxed her hands, her knees, and watched him for a while, turning the pages, resting on one, moving his lips, turning again, reading . . .

She stood up.

He still didn't look up.

She looked at the top of his head, at the empty cup by his feet, at his oversized Bible. And she felt nothing. No guilt. No fear. Just freedom. She walked out of the room. She didn't think he noticed her leave.

Twenty-seven

       Summer, such as it was, came and went. Now Joy stood by her bedroom window watching the leaves fall from the horse-chestnut tree.

Esmine watched her for a while. 'Get on with it Joy. Stop day-dreaming,' she said eventually.

'I was just thinking that I may have overdone it Essy.'

'I have been thinking that since I saw all these barrels. You must be shopping for a lifetime.'

'I'm not. It's just that everybody seems to be asking for large items.'

'As I said,' Esmine sat on the floor wrapping clothes into small bundles for one of the barrels, 'you shouldn't have promised everyone on the island something.'

'It feels like that, doesn't it?'

'What time are they coming to pick them up?' Esmine scanned the barrels, trunks and boxes that littered the room.

'They'll be here at noon tomorrow.'

'Thank God, so I can have my free time back.'

'I'm pleased too. I'll be glad to get my room back again. There is just nowhere to walk.' She put the remaining items in the last of the barrels and fixed on the lid, putting the padlock in place. 'I have a vision of locking all these barrels and trunks and then losing the keys.'

'We did that once, didn't we? When we went to Trinidad. Do you remember?'

'Yes, we had to break the lock.'

'It took ages.'

There was a knock on the door.

Joy called out, 'Oh come in Janet. I don't know why you're knocking.'

Janet entered and looked around the room with a smile. 'Got through finally, Joy. They've collected the car. This morning.'

'Oh thanks, Jan. One down then.'

'Only a million barrels and trunks to go,' Esmine said gloomily.

'When *will* the crate get there Joy?'

'The guy told me six weeks, so in theory it should get there a couple of weeks before me.'

'Will that be all right?' Janet asked, kneeling on the floor next to Esmine.

'I hope so. What I'm dreading is all the hassle I'm going to have getting them released from customs.'

'And it's going to cost you a fortune,' Esmine said. She started to laugh.

Janet and Joy looked at each other.

'She's finally cracked up,' Joy said, smiling.

Esmine laughed, tried to speak, but laughed again.

'What's funny Esmine?' Janet smiled, her plump cheeks making her dimples more pronounced.

'I was just thinking of this old friend of our parents. You don't know her Janet. She used to live on our road when we were growing up – Mrs Ansell.' Esmine looked at Joy. 'I was just imagining your going home Joy with all the rubbish that she took when she moved home.'

Joy started to laugh too. 'Me? Like that woman? You must be crazy.'

Esmine told Janet the story. Mrs Ansell's husband had died

suddenly of a heart attack and she had come into what she considered to be a considerable amount of money. They had been insured on first death, and the money she received paid off the mortgage of their large Edwardian house in south London, as well as the house they had been paying for in Jamaica.

'Mrs Ansell was a really simple woman, one of those who had left Jamaica after spending all their lives working fields and praying for rain. She had hardly gone to school and could barely read and write,' Joy added. 'Daddy had looked after the business for her and she had moved home with her two daughters, who were younger than Esmine and me.' She looked at Esmine. 'When she had been there for, how long Esmine?'

'Two years.'

'Yes, two years . . .'

'. . . We went to visit her. We couldn't believe it. Before she left she'd dragged us around London *buying up*, as she called it. We knew she'd bought another set of everything she had in the house. You name it – settees, coffee table, glass cabinet, fridge, freezer – everything! But we thought she would have given the old ones away. Anyone would. Who would have thought that she would have kept everything?'

'Kept everything?' Janet stretched out her legs and rubbed them.

'Kept everything,' Joy and Esmine said together.

'When we got there, it was baking hot, as it is in August in Jamaica. Esmine you were fussy about your hair as usual and slapping mosquitoes that weren't there.'

'That's your version,' Esmine said.

'Seriously,' Joy continued, 'we were hot, and going into that house made us hotter. She took us for a tour. In the sitting room there were two clashing sets of settees, two coffee tables from different times – you know the glass-topped patterned ones from the sixties – and the stacking formica ones. Two glass cabinets, two Jesus and the disciples at the Last Supper on opposite sides of the room. In the dining room it was the same, two fridges, two freezers, two cookers . . .'

'Never!'

'Yes Janet, I am telling you.'

Janet frowned, 'How ridiculous. Why?'

'Up to this day I have never been able to work it out and Mummy wouldn't let me ask her.' Joy laughed.

'*Nobody* wanted you to ask her Joy, because we know what you are like. Daddy made one or two jokes but I don't think she got them. So we all sat and roasted for the two hours we were there.'

'I couldn't believe it when we got to the bedrooms and there was space to walk. There was only one bed in each of the first three rooms . . .' Joy continued.

'. . . But when we got to the fourth, *four* beds were stacked in it!'

Janet and Esmine threw themselves at each other and laughed.

When they stopped, Joy shook her head, 'There is a funny side but I felt sick and angry afterwards. All that waste when there is so much poverty.'

'I suppose it is a bit greedy.' Janet tried to suppress more threatening laughter.

'And it was sad that she went on and on about not being able to get cornflakes and baked beans,' Esmine said.

'She didn't,' Janet stared at Esmine.

'Yes, she did.' Esmine eyes widened, 'She kept saying that her kids, poor little fat things they were then . . .'

Joy couldn't help smiling again.

'. . . Didn't like this and that, and that to please them she had to go to Miami to stock up . . .'

'With cornflakes and baked beans?' Janet said, disbelieving.

'By the looks of things, because when she opened up those barrels for us to see, there was mainly tinned stuff and packets of cornflakes.'

Janet shook her head, 'It's incredible!'

'And do you remember, Esmine, she went on about the second house she had bought and how much trouble she had getting the rent?'

'Yes, and while we were there she tried to evict someone who had missed a couple of weeks' rent. That woman is amazing. Are you going to see her when you get there?' Esmine smiled at her sister.

'I suppose I will have to, but thank God she's miles away from where I'm going. I can't stand greed . . .'

For a moment, they sat and looked at each other.

It was Esmine who broke the silence. 'So the house will be ready at the end of October?'

'Yes, so the agent said and Ben, you remember that very distant cousin from Redhills, he'll be staying in it until I get there.'

'That's the house your parents bought is it?' Janet asked.

Joy glanced at Esmine, 'Yes. It's a bit big for my purposes. Daddy expected four of us there but . . .' She sighed, '. . . It wasn't to be. I just hope he'll be satisfied, wherever he is, with just me.'

Janet and Esmine exchanged glances.

'I hope they *both* will be . . . I really hope so,' Esmine said.

'So you'll keep both houses? This one here and that?' Janet asked.

Joy and Esmine's eyes met.

It was Joy who answered, 'Yes, until circumstances change for one or other of us. But that will be a long way in the future, eh Essy?' she asked gently.

'So you say at the moment Joy. But you're right, there is no pressure. We can never say Mummy and Daddy didn't provide for us.'

'No, we can never say that. They were insured to the hilt. They must have known.'

Again Esmine broke the silence. 'So you told the senior partner at last eh?' Her voice was carefully even.

'Yes. I'd said I would tell him when it was exactly two months to go. So I went in this morning and told him. I thought, I have half-day off, I'll tell him and leave him with it to buzz through the offices.'

'What did he say?' Esmine sat back on her heels.

'Not much really. He is one of these stiff-upper-lip types so it's hard to get through to him.

'When I sat facing him across that antique mahogany desk of his, I thought, if I told this man I was moving him and his desk intact to Outer Mongolia he wouldn't shift a muscle. He'd just nod his head and say, *Jolly good* . . .' She smiled, 'He just went on about what a loss it was going to be to the practice and to him personally. God knows why.

'I sat and listened to him but I was thinking all the time that he would have been the first to stand in my way. He'd have given someone less qualified, less experienced than me, the most prestigious and lucrative work. Then he would eloquently articulate a hundred and one reasons why, after twenty years in the same position, I'd been passed over for promotion as many times.' Joy thought for a moment. 'So I felt triumphant as I sat telling him that I was going, because I knew I had got there before him and there was nothing he could do.'

She rubbed her hands together '. . . I thought, he doesn't after all have the total power he felt he had. It was a brilliant feeling.'

'So that's it then?' Esmine said, averting her eyes.

'Yes. That's it Sis. That is really it.'

Twenty-eight

Joy woke up, untangled herself from Lee's arms and slid out of the bed. She looked back at him. Not wanting to wake him up, she carefully pulled out her exercise clothes drawer, taking out the first pair of tracksuit bottoms and T-shirt that caught her eye. She crept into the bathroom, put them on and went downstairs.

After exercising, Joy stayed in the corpse position for a little longer than usual before lifting herself, without using her hands, off the floor.

In the kitchen she opened a bottle of mineral water, added half a squeeze of lime and meandered back to the sitting room.

It didn't get better. They had gone to the cemetery every month for over two years but each time the pain felt fresh. Esmine, especially, didn't seem to be healing. And in the last few months it seemed to Joy that new wounds were opening.

Esmine came downstairs to find her sister sitting with her legs tucked under her bottom, sipping her water.

'Morning.'

'Hi Esmine.'

Esmine kissed her on the forehead. 'Had a good sleep?' She sat next to Joy.

'Not really. I went to sleep with Lee droning on in my ear about losing me to a country, and woke up . . .'

'Having to go to the cemetery?'

'Yeah. I never sleep the night before we go anyway.' Joy sighed and put her glass down, 'Esmine do you think you should still go when I leave? You get so upset . . .'

'I have to Joy. I need to go.' Tears welled up in her eyes.

'Okay, Essy, don't get upset now.' Joy stretched out her legs.

'I know that they aren't there Joy, but I just need to go back . . .'

'Sure. Sure . . .' She tried to speak gently, 'I always feel extremely lonely before I go. This morning when I came down here, I felt like I was the only person left in the world.'

Esmine moved closer to her sister and rested her hand on her lap. 'Every time I go it's as if they died yesterday. I see us sitting here waiting for the cortège to come. I see the procession around their opened coffins in the church. I see them shovelling earth over them . . . I try to get it out of my system Joy but I can't . . . I thought I would after all this time. I thought I could . . .' She started to cry.

Joy rested her arm around her shoulders.

'Essy, Essy, please.'

Esmine wiped her eyes.

'When I go, if you do have to go, will you ask Janet to go with you?'

Esmine bit her lips. 'I don't know Joy. I don't know if I want to . . . if she'll understand.'

'Just to go with you in the car. You could ask her to wait in the car for you. You can go to the tombs by yourself.'

Esmine sniffled. 'I suppose I could ask her to do that.'

'I would feel better.'

'Joy, I don't know how I'm going to manage without you . . .' She sobbed desperately.

Joy pulled her closer.

'. . . I won't be able to manage. I won't . . . I know I won't. Everyone I really need is being taken away from me . . . What have I done to deserve it?'

Joy listened to her sobbing. It could have been two years ago

211

over again, with that policeman announcing their parents' deaths. Or that time when she first told Esmine she was going back. All she could do was to rock their bodies together.

So locked together were they that neither of them heard or saw Janet first and then Lee as they came into the room, concerned about the loud crying.

The two of them stood for a moment before Janet went to make a pot of tea.

Lee sat down beside Joy and tried to hold both of them.

The cemetery was off a dual carriage way, enclosed by trees. Joy turned in through the huge iron gates and drove into the car park. They took the flowers and entwined their hands as they walked to their parents' graves.

When they got there, they stooped together beside the graves, Esmine crying as Joy arranged the flowers first on one and then the other.

As usual Joy felt she had to try to smile, but her lips trembled and she couldn't steady them as she looked from one grave to the next. At her mother's and then her father's. Solemnly, she raised her hand to her mouth, pressed it against her lips, and waved it through the air.

In her heart of hearts she knew that if her father had anything to do with it, the kiss would not connect under these cold grey skies but would have to float on across other skies for five thousand miles, then search until it found the place where his mother had buried his navel string.

The next thing she knew, she was smiling.

Esmine wasn't ready yet. Joy looked up and around the cemetery. A cortège was pulling up on the other side. It looked so lonely, just three cars.

At her parents' funeral, cars had blocked the roads outside the church on the way to the cemetery. These poor people in this country; as they live so they die. She looked down again at her father's grave as she recognised one of his sayings.

Esmine finally stood up. Joy entwined their hands as they walked back to the car. She knew that had Esmine been the one going away, Joy's visits would dwindle to once or twice a year. But Esmine would still go, once every month.

As Joy turned back on to the dual carriage way she felt an overwhelming pain. She could visualise Esmine, going back alone, month after month, to shed more tears on the already well-watered graves.

'Joy?'

'Mmm.' She slid the car into fourth.

'I think you are right. I'll ask Janet to come with me.'

'All the way?'

'All the way.'

'Oh Esmine, I'm glad.'

'It *will* be lonely otherwise . . . and Janet is like a sister.'

'Yes she is, isn't she?' Joy touched the scar under her chin. A shiver went through her body.

'Esmine?'

'Ummm.'

But Joy lost her nerve.

'What is it Joy?' Esmine's face was concerned.

'You know that evening on the way to the hospital, in the ambulance . . .' Joy had tried almost every day for the last year to tell her, but she had lost the courage each time. She had not known exactly how to put it. But now she knew she had to do it. There was only a month to go before she left. She cleared her throat. '. . . You know that evening when those blokes beat me up?'

Esmine turned to her and nodded.

'The strangest thing happened to me on the way to the hospital. In the ambulance . . .' As she spoke, her mouth was dry but her heart grew lighter.

213

Esmine stared at the side of Joy's face. '*What* Joy?'

'Esmine . . .'

She could feel Esmine's eyes.

'Go on.'

'Esmine, when I was in the ambulance, I saw Daddy . . .'

'Joy for God's sake! Daddy had been dead for months,' Esmine shouted, her hands shooting up to cover her ears.

'I know Esmine . . . I know . . . But I saw him.'

Esmine stared at her.

Joy stole a glance at her. 'Esmine, I need to tell you about it.' Esmine tensed her body and turned away. 'I don't want to hear, Joy. *I do not want to hear.*'

Joy continued anyway, knowing that Esmine couldn't walk away. 'I knew that I was conscious again because I was hurting all over.'

Esmine's face softened a little.

'. . . I remember the ambulance man holding my hand when I came round. I remember coughing up blood when I tried to speak . . .'

Esmine bit her lips, reached out and touched her sister.

'When I'd stopped coughing he rested me down again. I tried to open my eyes. Although they opened only as little slits. I knew they were open because I saw the ambulance man's face. I remember thinking how gentle he looked. So unlike the two faces I had just seen snarling at me, kicking hell out of me . . .

'He was sort of pinky but I didn't find him revolting. I just kept looking at his blue eyes, at his hand holding mine. Then I thought I must be hurting him because I could feel the pressure that I was applying to his hand.'

Joy stopped at the red lights and turned to look at Esmine. She found a smile for her before she turned again and pulled away.

'Then something made me look up . . . God! And there he was.'

'Joy, please! Please!'

'Yes Esmine. There he was! He was just standing there . . .' She touched her chin again. 'You know the way he would stand with his head cocked to one side and his lips slightly pouted?' Joy smiled then. 'Well he was standing there, just like that. He wasn't smiling and he wasn't serious. I reached out to touch him.'

The tears welled up in Esmine's eyes and ran down her cheeks.

'I reached out to touch him and the man with the pinky face and kind blue eyes sort of gently rested me back down . . .' Joy sighed.

'. . . But then, Esmine, he turned round suddenly, a puzzled look on his face, as if *he* felt something . . . You know when somebody is watching you and you can feel it?' She stopped talking and listened to her sister's breathing for a while.

'When he turned back to me, he shivered.'

'Joy. Oh Joy.' Esmine took a tissue from the dashboard and pressed it on to her eyes.

'But I couldn't touch him Essy. I couldn't make connection. So I thought, I'm going . . . He's come to take me. I felt so good. So light, so free for a short time.

'Then I saw the way he was looking at me. He had the deepest, saddest look I'd ever seen on his face.' Joy shook her head. 'It was then that I knew he wasn't going to take me with him. I was so upset.' Joy gripped the steering wheel.

'I thought if I told him how much I really hurt and that I didn't ever want it to happen to me again. That I didn't want to be here for it to happen to me, then he'd take me. But before I could speak, he reached out and rubbed his thumb, just like this . . .' She ran her thumb across the scar under her chin.

Esmine covered her mouth with her palm.

Joy bit her lips. 'His hand felt as it had always done . . . firm . . . warm . . . When he moved it away it had the blood on it, dried blood . . .'

Joy's legs were shaking so much she had to pull over and stop.

Esmine lent her head on her shoulder.

215

Joy smoothed her sister's hair back. 'Do you remember the night before he died, when he was telling us how proud he was of us?'

Esmine nodded.

'He suddenly had that same look of triumph on his face. And I thought, why does he look like that when he's not going to take me with him? I was so angry and kept trying to get up. But the ambulance man kept pushing me to lie down. I started to cry but Daddy shook his head and whispered, *Never cry about it . . , just do what you know you have to*. Esmine he sounded just the same.'

'Joy . . .'

Joy couldn't stop herself. 'So I stopped crying and he wasn't there any more . . . ' She stared vacantly through the windscreen.

They sat there in the car for a long time without speaking. Eventually Joy said, as she held firmly to Esmine's hand, 'I knew then Esmine that I *had* to go back. I had to smell the earth again, have children there, lots and lots of children with a real Jamaican man, die and be buried there and hope that some of my kids will do so too. Keep company,' she paused, 'with him and Mummy.'

Esmine stared at her.

'Yes Esmine! Mummy, Daddy and the other old people he always spoke about.'

And when at last Joy drove away she felt greatly relieved, because for the first time she had acknowledged aloud what she knew had really happened.

Twenty-nine

Joy's last week was not how she had imagined it would be. There were the get-to-gethers she had wanted. She cooked the curry goat she knew she would not eat, and fried the snapper she could not stomach. When everyone was laughing as she had asked, she was wishing that they would just be quiet and go, so that she could be alone. But each time they went she couldn't wait for the next evening when they would come again so she could at least avoid the constant tears in Lee's and Esmine's eyes.

Esmine took a week off work so she could be with her, and so did Lee. Only Janet continued with her part-time job. Since it was November they did not go for long walks in the park, but stayed in the sitting room instead, talking between long silences.

Joy tried to balance her time between them. But there were one or two evenings that week when she had to tell Lee to spend the first part of the night alone so that she could be with her sister.

When she was with him in that last week, she had to exercise a level of control over her tongue that she would not have believed was possible. Yet even when she was trying her hardest she couldn't help wanting to question him; to ask him about Loretta, whom she knew was now renting a room at his house. She tried to suggest that he should now look to buy his own place. She made to lash out, to criticise him, to tell him to grow up, to stand on his own two feet. To tell him that most men of his age did not live with parents and obnoxious sister. She thought about saying all of these things, but just stopped herself from saying any of them.

Perhaps she could not say them because the intensity of their relationship that week left her with little energy to do anything other than think. She had not imagined that it would be possible to continue with him right to the end. And it pained her, more than she had allowed herself to admit, that she had to lose him forever.

But his tears caused more pain than anything else that week. At times when their bodies rested from the ecstasy of their love she would reach up and find that it was not the perspiration of pleasure that she touched on his cheeks. When they were cooking, the third or fourth pot of curry goat that week, she would look up to see his heart-shaped lips and his pearl white teeth, but she would find him crying. It was too much for her to bear but, she knew, bear it she must.

And Esmine too, as in those weeks after their parents' deaths, would often be found crying in some secret corner.

But Joy knew there was nothing she could do to help them. The hunger for her homeland was in her blood, and the history went back too far. Back to the time when those who parented the whole of humanity controlled their own destiny. Then past that to the time of shackles, branding, raping and lynching, to the continual breaking of rock stone, to the working of barren grounds with corn that wouldn't grow, right up to the time when hundreds and thousands of people shook white handkerchiefs for those going away, to have the hell kicked out of them.

One night, after she had told Lee to sleep, she sat with Esmine late into the morning, and her sister told her how proud she was of her, how England's loss would be Jamaica's gain.

They talked of their childhood, of their parents. That night there was no rivalry, no bitterness or jealousy because they both understood that their differences were also their strengths.

The day before she was due to leave, the sisters went for the last time to the cemetery.

Joy kissed each of the two red roses they had brought, before gently putting each in place. But, unlike previous times, it was Esmine who now entwined their hands and supported her sister back to the car.

The night before she travelled the four of them sat together and talked until well into the morning.

'Esmine . . .', she told her sister, 'I'm glad you are staying. This country belongs to you . . . and you too Janet . . . and you too baby.' She rested back in Lee's arms. 'It's your country,' she said again with conviction.

'It's yours too Joy.' Lee managed to say.

'I think it belongs to all of us,' Esmine supported. 'It's funny, people here can't accept it. They talk of first-generation blacks, second-generation blacks. You don't hear them enumerating the generations of whites who live here.'

'That's true.' Joy was serious.

'I can still see them,' Esmine said, '. . . In the year three thousand, having a special department, with highly paid statisticians painstakingly enumerating the generations of blacks in England.' She sighed and looked around at her sister, at Lee, at Janet.

They nodded agreement.

'In one sense, I hope that there aren't many like me, of our generation, going back . . . People here should be made to move over, to accept our ownership of this country . . . our joint ownership.'

'They have no choice,' Lee said emphatically.

'It's our birthright,' Esmine added, meeting Joy's eyes.

Janet smiled grimly. 'A fact of life, whether they want to accept it or not. This will always be home for most of us.'

219

Later that morning car loads of family and friends found places in the short-stay car park at the airport. Joy's bags were slung on to a trolley. Her legs were weak but she had to run with her friends. It was a mad rush. She was late.

She kissed each of them in turn before falling upon her sister, whose eyes and smile, Joy felt, had never been more radiant. Squeezing their bodies together, Joy, surprised, smiled in return.

She moved away from the group with Lee. It was only then that she almost totally lost the strength in her legs.

Lee cried, and for one moment Joy feared that he would not release her to heed the final call to board the aircraft.

At passport control she forced herself to look back and respond to the waves and blown kisses. She picked out Esmine, standing arm in arm with Janet, still smiling sweetly at her. Joy looked again but could not see Lee.

She found her seat on the aircraft, tucked her hand luggage under her seat in front of her, fastened her seat belt and opened the note Lee had pressed in her hand as they had hugged for the last time.

Sweetheart! If in a year, you want me as much as I need you, whoever or whatever transpires between then, please let me know. I will live for your answer. Lee.

The cabin crew moved through the aircraft, checking seat positions and seatbelts.

Joy's body tensed as she waited for the most dreaded part of the flight, the taxi down the runway and the take-off. A smile crept across her face though. She read the note again, folded it, and tucked it into her passport holder.

As the aircraft manoevred into position, accelerated along the runway and lifted off, Joy cocked her head to one side and smiled. She could have sworn she could hear the humming bird sing.